THE INNOCENT WIFE

Brides of Little Creede, Book 3

CICI CORDELIA

SOUL MATE PUBLISHING

New York

THE INNOCENT WIFE

Copyright©2019

CICI CORDELIA

Cover Design by Syneca Featherstone

Published in the United States of America by
Soul Mate Publishing
P.O. Box 24
Macedon, New York, 14502

ISBN: 978-1-68291-898-2

ISBN: 978-1-68291-888-3

www.SoulMatePublishing.com

To the men in CiCi's life!

Okay, both halves of her life:

Pat Yeko, and Don Chaffin.

Without these two very patient, good-natured,

and supportive guys, BRIDES OF LITTLE CREEDE

might have eventually been written but the series'

creators would've been a frazzled mess.

Acknowledgments

A big 'Thank You' goes to Debby Gilbert, CiCi's hardworking and meticulous editor, who can look at a scene and know exactly what it needs, beyond those pesky commas all authors tend to forget. Her expertise and enthusiasm for BRIDES OF LITTLE CREEDE kept two crazed BFFs on track.

And to CiCi's readers who responded to each book so wonderfully, a super-big 'Thanks!' Because of you, Little Creede might just live on in another trilogy. Or two.

Chapter 1

Little Creede, Colorado
August, 1881

Heat shimmered off the new tin roof of the jailhouse. With no breeze to speak of, the closer Sheriff Joshua Lang got to the front of the building and its overhanging portico, the more he sweated. He whipped off his hat and blotted his damp forehead. Time to open all three windows and pray for wind.

He unlocked the heavy wooden door and stepped inside. Unclipping his double holster, he hung it on a nail embedded in the wall behind his desk and took care of the windows before he dropped into the lumpy old chair he swore he'd replace one of these days. Wasn't going to be today, for certain. Or next week or even next month, judging by how busy he'd found himself lately.

His town was growing, and not always in a good way. Joshua had dreaded the day Little Creede started behaving like a boom town, and that day had most definitely arrived. As he scraped his damp hair off the back of his neck to help the cooling process along, he peered out the side window, eyeing the fancy new building at the very edge of town, past Doc Sheaton's office. From here, he could see the scrolled frontage and a corner of the sign with the lettering 'Gleason's Gambling Galleria' painted in bold red.

The structure had gone up pretty fast, with a grand opening occurring later in the month. According to the local rumor mill, its owner had come in on the midweek stage from Silver Cache, stood seven feet tall, boasted orange hair, and had been seen only once outside the newly-painted Galleria. Joshua figured that wild of a physical description must've been exaggerated somewhat. He had to admit, though, he was damned curious.

Townsfolk saw welcome revenue coming from such a sprawling gamblers' establishment, as well as trouble. It was Joshua's job to see that the revenue outweighed the trouble.

His all-encompassing sweep of the main thoroughfare took in Loman's Mercantile and Millie's Milliners, nestled side by side and newly whitewashed, though Silas Loman would have to reapply the lime mixture within the year. For now, in the sun, the buildings shone. A thrilled Betsey Loman had given her red-faced husband a big, smacking kiss of thanks right on the sidewalk in front of several folks who'd make sure to tease poor Silas for weeks. Probably months.

The Miner Stage House flanked the nearest corner, its wide porch and polished rockers inviting a person to sit a spell and enjoy the day. From an upper open window Joshua caught a rich, womanly laugh that could only belong to Lucinda Carter, his best friends' mother and the Stage House's hostess-manager. An answering murmur, deep and rough, blended briefly and abruptly cut Lucinda off in mid-chuckle. Grinning widely, Joshua kicked back in his chair, clasping his hands behind his head.

Sounds like Dub's getting himself a bit of afternoon delight. We should all be so lucky.

Joshua then glanced beyond the Stage House, to the opposite corner where a short trail led to Little Creede's schoolhouse. As if conjured out of his wishful thinking, the door swung open and Vivian Carter stepped out onto the stoop, dark hair shimmering in the sun, carrying a broom.

Speaking of trouble.

Petite and dainty, dressed in something yellow, the sight of Harrison and Frank Carter's little sister always clutched deep within Joshua's heart. As far as he was concerned, the girl was forever beyond his reach.

Too innocent. Too lovely. Too . . . endearingly virtuous. And young, by God. So young. In years as well as in life experiences. Sometimes Joshua felt a hundred instead of a birthday shy of thirty.

He swung his chair away, determined to put thoughts of Vivian out of his mind. Easiest way to do that was to vacate his office and go looking for some kind of rabble to squash.

He'd risen and strode to the door when it burst open, the latch slamming into the wall. Joshua found himself confronting a bear of a man with a wild, carroty mane of curls, dressed in the fanciest duds he'd ever seen.

The newest citizen of Little Creede, without a doubt. Maybe not seven feet tall, but definitely red-haired. The gent's suit coat stretched across massive, burly shoulders and his striped black and gray trousers broke their cuffs over shiny, silver-tipped boots. He held a feathered derby in one beefy hand and stuck the other out toward Joshua, who regarded it warily.

"Yew the law 'round heah?" Before Joshua could respond, the man grabbed his hand and pumped it eagerly. "Ah've been meanin' to stop by. Knight Gleason's the name. From Atlanta, bless 'er soul. Got in the other day. Ah'm the proud owner of Gleason's Gamblin' Galleria." He swept his derby expansively toward the open doorway. "Ah always find it good business sense to acquaint mahself with the local law enforcement."

"All right." Joshua wasn't sure what else to say. Mister Gleason's booming voice nearly rattled the glass from the windows. Larger than life and at least six inches taller than

Joshua—who by no means considered himself puny—the man dominated the room. "Welcome to Little Creede, Mister Gleason." He indicated the only extra chair in the room. "Have a seat."

"That lil' thang?" Gleason barked out a laugh that echoed like a shotgun blast. "Why, if'n ah set mahself down, ah'll bust it into kindlin'. How's about ah situate heah instead." Gleason leaned against the doorjamb and Joshua swore the wood groaned in protest. He managed to retain polite interest as the town's newest businessman barreled on. "Ah'm about ready to open mah doors, yessir. Gamin' on the first floor an' some fancy rooms above, fer those wantin' to sleep it off an' start fresh in the mornin'. Got mah grand openin' date all set an' wanna issue yew a personal invite to come on by. First round's on the house."

"Well, I—"

"Put yew up in a real straight game, too. Yew look like a pokerin' man, Sheriff. Fairest tables in the land of silver." Gleason nodded vigorously. "Ask anyone around, Knight Gleason plays fair an' square."

"I'm sure you do, but—"

The man rolled over Joshua like a runaway steam engine. "Ah doan' allow cheatin', nosir. Not a mark on mah decks, y'heah? Y'all come an' see fer yerself. Bring yer friends. Drink's on me." He lowered his voice to a rumble. "Now, ah got somethin' to ask. Y'see, ah got mahself a load of silver an' if'n yew'd point me toward yer bank, ah'd be right grateful." His bright blue eyes narrowed to suspicious slits. "Yew got a bank in these parts, ain'tcha?"

"That we do." Fascinated with the newest townie and his blustering ways, Joshua retrieved his hat. "Matter of fact, I'm about to make my afternoon rounds. I'd be glad to escort you to First Commerce Bank." He dropped his Stetson in place and adjusted the rim. "Our head bank teller will assure you've got everything you need. Miss Hannah Penderson. I'll introduce you."

"Hannah, huh? Well, now, that's a purty name. An' she's a miss?" Gleason's bushy red eyebrows actually waggled as he made for the door on surprisingly graceful feet.

"She's a sweetheart, Mister Gleason. A small, delicate lady." Joshua followed Gleason out the door and nodded down the dusty street. "This way."

Gleason fell into step beside him. "Small an' delicate, y'say? Well, now. That's just the way ah like mah women."

~ ~ ~

"Be back in an hour, Nate," Vivian called, as the young boy burst outside, hurrying off for his supper.

"I will. Thank you, Miss Vivian," he hollered. The school door slammed behind him, shaking on its hinges.

Making a mental note to have one of her brothers tighten up the bolts, Vivian finished sweeping off the wooden sidewalk leading to the trail offsetting schoolhouse land from the rest of the main thoroughfare. Envisioning wildflowers filling in the gaps between walkway and grass, she decided to take Nate up on his offer—well, he'd actually begged—to help her plant and then care for the tiny seedlings she nurtured in a shaded spot behind the school. Though all the children took an interest in horticulture, Nate was by far the most enthusiastic.

She couldn't be more proud of him if he were her own.

A strong yearning overtook her as she paused in her sweeping and stared toward the outskirts of town where Nate's foster parents, the Wilkeys, currently lived. The boy had been dealt a hard hand in life, his mother a whore who'd abandoned him, and his father an escaped criminal who'd been killed by Vivian's brother Frank after the man had shot Frank's wife. Thankfully, Catherine survived.

Now, Mark and Susan Wilkey had a babe of their own and could no longer afford to keep Nate. In another year he'd be of an age to apprentice, those opportunities limited to mining, blacksmithing, or further out West, ranching.

Slowly, Vivian carried the broom inside the schoolhouse, propping it against the storage cubby, then unrolled her sleeves and rebuttoned her cuffs. In the quiet room her thoughts bounced worse than a trapped canary in a timber box.

A local mining or smithy apprenticeship would be difficult enough for a young boy, but the thought of Nate traveling so very far from town to work long, hard hours in an unfamiliar place, with tough, wild cowboys . . .

Her heart clenched with sorrow. It didn't bear contemplation. Oh, how she'd love to adopt him, if only she were a married woman.

"So unfair," she muttered to herself, crossing to her desk. A pile of schoolbooks sat neatly in the center. She'd asked Nate to choose his subjects for their tutoring sessions, and he'd followed her instructions as precisely as the books, stacked and waiting for her. Later, he'd carry them back to his room at the Wilkey's place, and probably study well into the night.

Two days a week she stayed in town a few hours longer, working with Nate, feeding his eager thirst for knowledge. As wonderfully as Susan and Mark treated him, neither had any book knowledge and could barely read. The boy was so intelligent, and Vivian could see him attending university back East. Taking it upon herself to supplement Nate's schooling had been the best decision all around. Though class had only been in session ten days, she'd already been tutoring Nate for a month.

She spread out the books, taking note of his weekly picks. Literature. Arithmetic. She hefted a tome at the bottom of the stack and stared at the title. "Good heavens, Latin?"

She set it down, bemused at the thought she might have to brush up herself, since she had studied Latin while still in grade school.

Quite the variety we'll have. The notion delighted her. And it was never too early to start learning a language.

She collected her hat and stepped to the washstand, peering into the cloudy mirror nailed to the wall and securing the honey straw in place. Smoothing a stray curl, she found her thoughts darkening with worry. Nate's ninth birthday had already passed. If no one took him in he'd have to apprentice by age ten. The laws varied from place to place which meant as early as six months from now, he could be sent off with no choice in location or trade.

Unless she could find a way to prevent it. Her brothers would do their best to secure a good place for Nate, though he might have to leave Little Creede for heaven only knew where.

Maybe the time had come to sit both Frank and Harrison down, make them understand her concern.

Sighing, Vivian slipped her purse-strings over her wrist and crossed to the door. After a light meal with her mother over at the Stage House, she'd return to spend a precious hour with Nate.

As she reached for the latch, the door abruptly swung open. Blinking in confusion, Vivian registered the bearded, hatless young man swaying in the doorway, wearing a silly grin and grimy clothes. When the stench of whiskey fumes wafted close enough for her to inhale, she wrinkled her nose. The man was utterly soused.

As she stood there, frozen, unable to fathom what to do, he lurched over the threshold and stumbled right into her, his hands landing on her bodice. Red-rimmed, muddy brown eyes looked her over with drunken boldness as he leered. "Hey, honey, how 'bout a kiss?"

His open mouth swooped in, tobacco-stained teeth and all. Rearing back, she fisted both hands and pushed against his grasp as her lips parted on a sharp, piercing scream.

~ ~ ~

Two blocks from the jail, Joshua took off running, yanking on his right-hand holster, narrowed eyes trained in the direction of the schoolhouse where a shrill, female shriek still echoed in the air. This time of day only one woman would be so naive as to linger at the edge of town by herself, where anything could happen.

Vivian Carter. Putting on a burst of speed, Joshua leapt over the bumpy ground where the walkway ended, and tore up the slight hill toward the schoolhouse, cursing as a second cry built, then choked off.

As if someone had clapped a hand over a mouth to shut them up.

"Christ." He jumped over three steps and erupted through the door in time to bring up an arm and point his Colt at the scraggly stranger who held a struggling Vivian against the wall with a hand covering her mouth. Unable to think straight, he aimed above the bastard's head and squeezed off a shot. The bullet lodged itself in an upper corner of one of the blackboards, shattering the slate.

The cretin froze, then dropped Vivian and backed away, hands in the air. "Don't shoot! I jes' wanted a lil' kiss."

Joshua rushed him before he could sidle out the door, leveling him with a solid punch to the jaw. The stranger hit the floor as Joshua shoved the muzzle of his gun to his throat. "Move and you're dead."

The need to break every bone in the bastard's body throbbed in his blood, but commonsense as a lawman won out. Pinning him down with one knee, he twisted the man's hands behind his back and clipped on restraints. He'd begun carrying them in anticipation of the kind of trouble boom towns seemed to attract.

Then his attention locked on Vivian and a growl rumbled in his chest as he took in her disheveled clothes and drooping hat.

Some of her soft brown hair had come loose, and there was no missing the fear on her face. When he spotted two dark, palm-shaped smudges on the front of her pretty yellow dress, rage boiled up inside him.

The man dared to put his filthy hands on her.

Noting the sheen of tears in her eyes, it took all of his control not to pull her into his arms and comfort her. "Did he hurt you?" he gritted out.

A slight tremble shook her shoulders, though her voice held firm. "No. He's mostly drunk."

"Yeah." Joshua turned back to his prisoner and repositioned his Colt at heart-level. Leaning in to bare his teeth, he cocked the hammer and took grim satisfaction at the way the man's face turned sickly white under the unkempt beard. "Who are you?"

"Guh, uh," was the only response he got.

Swearing impatiently, Joshua jabbed hard with the gun muzzle. "You're under arrest."

The idiot finally located his voice. "Nuthin', honest, I dint do nuthin'," he babbled.

"Wrong answer." Joshua grabbed his prisoner by the collar and hauled him to his feet just as Ben Parsons rushed through the door, gun drawn.

"I heard a— Shit, what's goin' on?" Ben's rounded eyes bounced from Vivian, visibly upset, to the bullet hole in the blackboard, to the grumbling figure straining against Joshua's hard grip.

"I'll explain later." He thrust his captive toward Ben. "Do me a favor and lock this bastard in a cell. You know where the key is."

"Sure thing, Sheriff." Ben kept his pistol trained steady as he dragged the slurring, protesting man out the door. "Shut up and walk. If you did what I think you did then you're one stupid son-of-a-bitch . . ." The rest of Ben's words were lost as the door swung shut behind him.

For a moment Joshua stood there, staring at the rough-hewn pine, striving hard to calm down as his anger churned deep.

At the asshole who'd attacked her.

At Vivian for putting herself in harm's way, regardless of the fright she'd experienced. If she were his woman, he'd make sure she wouldn't choose so foolishly.

But she's not my woman. She'll never be my woman, and I have no right to tell her what to do.

Vivian Carter deserved a better man than him. Like Nate, Joshua had been raised around whores, one of them his own mother, in a seedy Texas bordello outside of Galveston. But unlike Nate, who'd hung on to some of his innocent shine, Joshua lost his at the ripe age of four when he'd watched a vicious cowpoke beat his ma to death while he'd cowered in a corner.

No, he would never be good enough for Vivian Carter, no matter how much she tempted him.

Several bracing breaths later, he turned as she retrieved a pair of gloves from her desk to tug them on, as if preparing for a leisurely stroll to church. The overall image was ruined by those dark handprints, marring the gentle swell of her breasts.

Fresh fury blasted his temper all to hell. Stomping to her side, he loomed over her and rasped out, "Where do you think you're going?"

"To early supper." Eyes downcast, Vivian smoothed each finger into place, but Joshua didn't miss the way her hand shook. "Then I have a tutoring session back here, with Nate." She snatched her shawl off the desk and slung it around her shoulders. Frustration nearly choked him when she started for the door.

Damned stubborn woman.

Joshua snaked out a hand and nabbed her wrist. "Is that right? Don't think I'm letting you stay here with only a kid for protection." He spun her around, and it was like a punch in the gut when a single tear rolled down her cheek. "You *are* hurt."

Vivian wrenched her arm away, taking him by surprise. "I'm not hurt." She swiped at the dampness on her cheek. "I'm"—her voice wobbled—"m-mad that man thought he could take liberties. He was no gentleman."

"Of *course* he's not a gentleman," Joshua shouted, surging forward, thrusting his face close to hers.

All the harm that could have come to her if he hadn't been close enough to hear her cry out burned across his mind, and he curled his hands into fists to keep from shaking some sense into her. "These days half the men in this damned town are animals, ruffians who spend their spare time getting drunk and chasing skirts. Catching them, too, whether the woman wants it or not." He flung an arm toward the open doorway. "And now we've got a gambling galleria, to boot."

Her eyes shimmered with more tears, knocking away most of his anger. Heaving a sigh, he modulated his voice as best he could. "You need to understand, the town's growing fast. Along with growth comes danger. New people pouring in that we don't know, like that son-of—uh, that idiot I just locked up. It's my job to protect Little Creede and its townsfolk, and that includes you. Wait here while I collect my wagon and I'll escort you home."

"I'm not going home." Vivian snatched her handbag off the floor where it had fallen.

Joshua narrowed his eyes. "You're going straight home where you belong." All his efforts to remain in control of his temper flew out the window. Before she could rush outside, he caught her by the shoulder. "Damn it, Vivian—"

"Let. Go." She whirled around, her expression rife with feminine ire. "And don't cuss at me. I'm not a child and I'm not your daily chore, Sheriff Lang." She slapped his hand away. "I'm going to have a quick meal at Catherine's place and then I plan on spending an enjoyable hour or so tutoring Nate before I head home, and you can't stop me!"

Before he could grab her again, she stomped down the steps and tore along the walkway toward Main Street, leaving him stewing over her utter disregard for her own safety.

Chapter 2

One hand on her head to keep her hat from flying away, the other clutching her shawl closed, Vivian hurried down the dusty main street of Little Creede. The relentless late-afternoon sun blazed down, her undergarments already clinging damply to her skin. Hot anger simmered in her stomach like a kettle of boiling water. Perspiration beaded her forehead, a few drops trickling down her cheek.

Reality began to settle in, along with a sense of loss for something she never truly had. She'd dreamed of someday being courted by Joshua Lang, a man she'd been smitten with from the moment she'd stood in the middle of a crowded ice cream social at the Stage House and looked into his piercing hazel eyes. Nobody else seemed to exist, though townsfolk had swarmed around her. To this day she wondered how on earth her brothers had missed that first, intense connection between her and Little Creede's dedicated—and so very handsome—sheriff.

But Joshua would never truly see her as anything more than Harrison and Frank Carter's little sister. Which she'd soon discovered made her untouchable to most of the menfolk in town.

At least those with half a brain. She snorted. If her brothers found out how that cowpoke barged into the school to accost her, they'd most likely string him up.

"Where you goin' in such an all-fired hurry, missy?" Buck Adams called from the front porch of the boardinghouse he owned with his wife, Maude.

Vivian paused, releasing the hold on her hat to toss the elderly gentleman a friendly wave. His failing health had them all worried, and hoping to brighten his day, she often stopped by for a chat, sitting next to him in one of the sun-bleached visitin' rockers. If he felt up to it, they'd play checkers, the wily old codger blatantly cheating and Vivian often laughing too hard at his antics to protest.

Though Buck and Maude were fun to visit with, they both gossiped notoriously to each other and often half the town, so Vivian had learned to guard her tongue when around either of them.

She managed a smile. "The Stage House, for supper and maybe one of Betsey's fancy little desserts before they're all gone."

The words no sooner passed her lips, when strong hands gripped her shoulders and gently spun her around, until she stared into the eyes of the one man she desired but could never have.

"It's not safe for a young woman to be running around town unescorted." The velvet rasp of Joshua's voice curled along her ear. His palms slid down to her upper arms and held firm.

Being this close to him, after already dealing with him once at the schoolhouse, shot a thrill straight through her. Evening breezes off the Lower Cascades blew his long, golden-brown hair around his broad shoulders, and she could only stare. He was so ruggedly masculine, so very male and . . . so *everything*, her heart had a hard time letting go of her dream.

Buck's scratchy chuckle pulled her out of her daze, and she groaned. The way gossip spread in this town, everyone would soon hear about how the schoolteacher went all moon-eyed over Sheriff Lang, right in front of the boardinghouse.

Just another reason for folks around here to treat me like a child.

With a huff of frustration, she spoke politely, forcing the words past clenched teeth. "Sheriff, there's no reason for you to be concerned. I'll be perfectly safe with Catherine."

Her sister-by-marriage, and owner of The Miner Stage House, could more than take care of herself. Vivian knew of at least two weapons the woman carried on her person at all times, and she had deadly aim. Catherine wouldn't need a man to save her.

The thought shamed Vivian, making her more determined than ever to show the aggravating man standing before her she'd changed greatly from the shy young miss who'd arrived in Little Creede a year ago.

Determination to be more like Catherine straightened Vivian's spine. She no longer resided in genteel Ohio, constrained by a rigid set of rules men considered proper for a lady.

Her tension eased, and her chin tilted up. No, she lived in a brand-new state now. Colorado's wild, western openness would let her spread her wings and push her boundaries to enjoy all life had to offer.

I'm done trying to meet everyone's expectations.

Joshua frowned as their eyes met. Could he read her defiant refusal to be cowed?

"I'll walk you over," he said as if it were a foregone conclusion, "and you stay put until one of your brothers can take you home."

"Don't be silly." She twisted in an attempt to shrug him off, but his grip only tightened. "Please let go, you're causing a scene."

As she'd dreaded, townspeople were noticeably taking an interest in the spectacle of them arguing. With a low curse Joshua lifted his head and glowered at those nearby, including Buck and Maude who'd ambled over to the railing, nosy as usual. "Nothing to see here, folks. Go about your business."

Heads bent guiltily, some at least trying to appear as if they weren't blatantly eavesdropping. Vivian sighed. They'd be the talk of the town until something new came along for them to gossip about.

Thankfully she spotted Robert, her best friend and Dub Blackwood's nephew. Only a year or so older than her, Robert was a close confidante. Yanking one arm free, Vivian raised her hand to catch his attention as he strode across the street. "Robert, hello. Care to join me for supper at the Stage House?"

Robert's face split into a grin as he approached, his dark eyes sparkling with amusement. Their friendship had cemented one night when, depressed over her infatuation with Joshua, she'd shared her feelings with Robert who suffered his own romantic troubles. At the time, he'd lamented over a woman in town, three years his senior and affianced to a businessman in Silver Cache.

Gaining the front stoop of the boardinghouse, he crooked an elbow. "Sure, Viv. Would love to." He nodded politely to Joshua. "Sheriff."

Joshua's mouth flattened. The sound of an approaching stagecoach finally attracted the attention of the remaining gawkers. Tense moments passed, and Vivian wondered if Joshua would release her without further argument, when his grip loosened.

Finally, you frustrating man.

She turned to Robert and took his arm. Even though the sheriff wasn't aware of her feelings toward him, the part of her still angry at him demanded he understand she was a full-grown woman. On impulse she rose on tiptoe and pressed a kiss to Robert's clean-shaven cheek, appreciating the faint soap scent clinging to his skin.

A growl sounded from Joshua.

Her stomach flipped with renewed hope at the look in his stormy gaze. Anger and desire stared back at her, and for the first time since meeting him, Vivian considered the possibility that she might have a chance with the sheriff after all.

~ ~ ~

It took a great deal of constraint on Joshua's part not to pull his gun on Robert as the young miner glanced at him with an amused expression that said, *I've got her affection, you ass. What are you going to do about it?* Though Joshua knew the two were more friends than sweethearts, jealousy burned through him from that one small kiss she'd placed on Robert's cheek.

She's not mine. Best not to forget that.

Berating himself did nothing to stop the contrary voice in his head. But Vivian's safety had to be his top priority, not his feelings for her that he'd never act upon.

Irritated, he gave in and urged, "Don't let her out of your sight, Blackwood, until her brothers show up for her."

Her rosy lips thinned. "Don't concern yourself, Sheriff." She tugged on Robert's arm. "Come on, let's go."

But Robert didn't budge, his focus sharpening on Joshua. "Why? What happened?"

Vivian waved a dismissive hand. "Nothing of importance."

"Some drifter attacked her at the schoolhouse," Joshua stated flatly.

"He was drunk," Vivian hastily added, "and he only wanted a kiss. I don't think he meant me any harm."

"Where is he?" Robert's voice rumbled with fury. He curled an arm around Vivian's shoulders and protectively drew her in tighter. "I'm gonna kill him."

"I had Ben lock him up, but—" Joshua broke off as he glimpsed Florence Johnson, Slim Morgan's favorite whore, and mother to Nate, sashay down the plank leading away from the carriage-station.

What's she doing back in town?

The woman had never been a beauty, but for a lusty miner she'd hold a definite appeal. Though dressed nicely, even pretty clothes couldn't hide the hard look in her eyes or the downturn of her narrow lips. Her voluptuous figure was corseted into a dark red traveling suit, and her drab brown hair had been swept to the side where a tiny, feathered excuse for a hat clung tenaciously. Joshua knew she'd once been much sought-after and probably considered the most adventurous whore for miles around.

Inside she was bitter and spiteful and dangerous. Joshua didn't want her anywhere near Nate. He'd grown mighty fond of the boy. A strong sense of protectiveness gripped him hard. He wasn't about to let this woman get her hands on that child.

Vivian glanced over her shoulder. "Who's that?"

Robert stared. "Isn't that Nate's mother?"

"Yes," Joshua bit out.

Though some of the women who'd worked at The Lucky Lady Saloon cleaned up their ways and now held decent jobs—thanks to Catherine after she'd turned the saloon into the Stage House—he doubted Florence had the backbone for such a life-altering transformation. Not after hearing of some of the debauchery she'd engaged in while employed by Slim Morgan.

"What?" Vivian exclaimed, her hand rising to her heart, worry evident in her voice.

Joshua knew she'd learned about Nate's mother from her brothers' wives, Retta and Catherine. And Vivian cared for Nate most of all, the two sharing a common fascination for science and poetry. If she were a married woman, she'd make Nate a wonderful mother.

The mere thought of her wed to someone sent a fresh surge of red-hot jealousy rushing through him.

Florence motioned to them, as if they were on friendly, speaking terms. Lifting the hem of her skirts off the dusty street, she hurried their way.

"Sheriff Lang," she called out, "I must speak with you."

He didn't miss the way Vivian clutched Blackwood's shirt, nor the man's returning squeeze of comfort. Joshua's jaw ticked, but he forced his gaze away from the two and back to Florence.

"Please, Sheriff." She stopped in front of him. "I'm looking for my boy. Nathanial. Can you tell me where I might find him?"

This woman had abandoned her son over a year ago, after Morgan went to prison and Catherine bought out The Lucky Lady, turning it into the finest eatery from here to Silver Cache. And well before Morgan's escape from Territorial, when he'd returned to Little Creede for vengeance and Frank Carter killed him.

Joshua wasn't about to let Florence come back now and ruin Nate's chances at a real life. Yet the odds of keeping him out of her clutches were diminished some, since the Wilkeys would soon no longer be able to foster the boy.

Before Joshua could intervene, Vivian stepped forward and with a jut of her chin faced off with Florence.

"What do you want with Nate?" She tensed as if expecting trouble, reminding him of a lioness determined to protect her young.

Vivian's natural vibrancy outshone Florence's worldly allure. Even the finest, most fashionable clothing couldn't hide the woman's brittle demeanor, nor the callousness that shone brightly in eyes the same color as the sky on a warm spring day.

They should have been beautiful. All Joshua saw was the ugliness inside the woman.

Florence's gaze swept over Vivian from head to toe with utter disdain. "What I want with *my* son is none of your business." Dismissing her, Florence turned her attention back to Joshua and plastered on the falsest of smiles. "I've come for Nathanial. Can you please get him for me?"

Vivian lunged forward, and Robert's arm wrapped around her waist, hauling her back. "You abandoned him," she spat, "and he's no longer any of your concern."

All pretense fell away, and the real Florence returned as she pivoted to pin Vivian with an icy glare. "Who the hell are you?"

Joshua placed himself between the women before they came to blows. "Robert, take Vivian to the Stage House while I have a talk with Miss Johnson."

Florence's insincere smile returned. "Why, Sheriff, there's no need for such formalities. Call me Florence. Or Flo, if you like. It's not as if we're strangers." She sidled closer and laid her hand on his chest, peeking up at him from under flirtatious lashes. "If you could fetch my boy, I'd be forever grateful."

The way she said 'grateful' left no doubt as to how she'd like to show her gratitude. Joshua's upper lip curled. *Hell no. Not now, not ever.*

Next to him, Vivian argued with Blackwood, loudly enough he could hear.

"Let *go*, Robert. This woman isn't getting her claws into Nate."

"Viv, let the sheriff handle this," Robert pleaded. "He'll do the right thing."

She actually snorted. "Will he? Seems to me they're well acquainted. Maybe he'll just hand Nate over."

Anger and disappointment tightened Joshua's shoulders. She actually believed he'd give the boy to this creature?

Pushing Florence's hand off his chest, he glanced Vivian's way with a raised brow, glad to see she at least had the decency to blush at her absurd statement.

Joshua had been fighting his feelings for Vivian Carter for the past year. He'd found her utterly sweet when she'd arrived in Little Creede with her mother; a girl blossoming into womanhood. Now she was astonishingly beautiful, with a soft creamy complexion and wide amber eyes in a captivating face that made a man think of satin sheets and stolen caresses. Dark, silky curls escaped her upswept hair and caressed high cheekbones above full pink lips that Joshua wanted to taste. Her petite figure showcased shapely curves his hands itched to stroke.

The interest in her gaze, whenever she looked at him, grew harder every day to ignore. And everything inside him rejected the way Blackwood hovered protectively by her side.

Yeah, I'm a jealous bastard. He had to keep reminding himself why she could never be his.

Frank and Harrison would cut out his heart if he touched her.

"Sheriff Lang," Florence snapped, her patience obviously waning. "I want my son. Now."

Joshua forced himself to refocus on the shrew in front of him. "That's not possible, ma'am. You gave up the right to Nate when you abandoned him."

She'd never been much of a mother before then, given the many bumps and bruises on Nate when Joshua had first arrived in town several years back when the boy was still very young. It wasn't until Joshua had a 'talk' with Florence, did the injuries become less in nature, though every now and then he'd spot fresh marks on the boy. Joshua figured Nate's clothing sometimes hid them. Sometimes, not.

Florence's eyes turned mean and her face scrunched into an unattractive portrait of belligerence. "Nathanial is mine, and you can't keep me from him."

With that threat hanging in the air, she spun away and stomped off.

Chapter 3

Four buildings down and around the corner, Florence Johnson leaned against a rear wall, breath heaving. Giving in to her temper, she stomped the heels of her half-boots into the ground.

Fury swirled in her chest and she wanted to scream but couldn't draw further attention to herself. She bit on her knuckles to keep herself quiet, and slowly regained her control.

Better.

Inhaling deeply, she straightened and paced in a tight circle, mindful of the activity on the other side of the building near a new milliners shop. Ladies tittered and chattered in the distance as a bell tinkled each time the door opened or closed.

It'd infuriated her when she'd spotted the sheriff hanging around. With no chance of getting past him without raising suspicion, she'd pretended to be a concerned mother.

Except the idiot hadn't bought it, not one bit.

She yanked out the pins holding her hat in place, flinging them aside, then ripped off the ridiculously beribboned thing. With a curse, she prepared to toss it into the muck her boots had churned up.

Arm raised to do just that, she paused. She couldn't afford to ruin a hat. Couldn't afford not to give at least the impression of being a well-heeled lady, though it galled her to do so.

No different than acting like I enjoyed it when a stinking customer bounced on my body and grunted in my ear.

With a final deep, calming breath, she smoothed the mangled felted wool and netting. Rooting around in a patch of flattened grass, she found one of the hatpins and stabbed it into the brim. Until she got her hands on Nathanial, she'd play the part.

Then she'd bring her boy home where he could do her the most good. It was her right, by God. She'd borne hours of pain bringing the little brat into this world, and he belonged to her.

Peering around the corner, Flo judged the distance to the stable behind the Lucky Lady. *Not the Lucky Lady any longer.* Cat Purdue turned it into some kind of fancy dining place, ruining the only home Flo had ever known, and the reason she'd left town in the first place. The songbird had always thought herself better than the rest of them. Now Cat had gotten herself married to Frank Carter. Jealousy ate at Flo to think on it. She used to have a real hankering for the big, handsome miner.

To hell with them all.

Once she secured a horse, she'd find Nathanial and hightail it out of town, shake the dust of this place off her boots once and for all.

Digging into the pocket of her walking skirt, she extracted her coin purse. She didn't have much left after purchasing a ticket to ride the stage from Silver Cache. She sure didn't want to waste any more on a return seat, but she couldn't stay in town.

Flo straightened, new determination flooding her.

I'll come up with a way to get my son, and nobody's gonna stop me.

~ ~ ~

Frank paced from one side of Catherine's pretty dining salon to the other. Standing near the lace-framed windows, Vivian eyed her brother with concern, not liking the look on his face. Gruff, rough, and wildly overprotective, Frank would most likely lock her in her room at the ranch to keep her out of harm's way even if the 'harm' in question wasn't more than some drunk already sitting in jail.

Yet, with Catherine's soothing influence, surely Frank had mellowed somewhat. *Rounded off a few of his crustier edges.* He pivoted and turned a fierce frown on her. Vivian shrank against the curtains, unable to control her reaction.

Better-rounded? Frank?

Not danged likely.

He strode across the room and pointed one finger at her, almost poking her in the nose. "You're staying at the ranch until further notice. That's final."

Anger crawled up her spine, helping her to stand tall. Vivian was sick and tired of being treated like a child, yet she had to fight the childish instinct to stomp her foot.

She swatted his hand away. "No, I'm not. I've got a job to do." Ignoring his low growl, Vivian appealed to their mother, seated at the dining table. "Mama, you understand, don't you? I have responsibilities."

"I know you do," Mama began, then gestured sharply at Frank when he opened his big mouth again. "Shut up, Frank. Your sister's a grown woman and she's right. She has a duty to this town's children."

"She can teach out at the ranch." This from Harrison, jumping in with an equally inane suggestion.

"Oh, for— An entire town full of children cannot trundle out to the ranch every day," Vivian sputtered, aghast at the thought. "Their parents would have fits, and what about chores before and after school? Not only that, I'm already escorted to and from town each day like some tot in diapers. It's mortifying and doesn't set a very good example for our future womenfolk."

She whirled at a slight cough from Catherine, who'd been pouring lemonade. "You know what I mean, Catherine. Our young females are growing up in a boom town. Don't you think they need to know how to take care of themselves?"

Mama nodded. "I agree. Catherine's been teaching me knife-throwing and handling—" When Frank started spouting curses, Mama stressed, "Yes, she has. She can also show your sister and anyone else who wants to learn."

"Like hell," Frank exclaimed, his cheeks actually paling. "A town filled with girls and women, all sporting knives or worse, pistols?"

"Yes, Husband. What about it?" Catherine slapped a glass into his hand. "Here. It's all you get this evening. I closed down the bar." She turned her back on his grumbling and stepped to Vivian's side, curling an arm around her waist. "Darling, I trained with knives for years. My reasons at the time were never in question, because I needed to protect myself as a woman alone in the world. Your situation is a bit different."

"I don't agree, Cath—"

"I'm not finished." Catherine gave her waist a squeeze. "Not every woman has two strong brothers to assist her, but this town grows daily. I'm less than thrilled to see a gambling casino opening soon, and I'd lay coins the man who assaulted you at the schoolhouse was one of the workers here to build that gaudy monstrosity." She swung a pointed glare between Frank and Harrison. "We have to be realistic where our town is concerned. Little Creede is getting bigger, and it doesn't hurt for the local women to learn how to handle a gun, those who've never tried."

"Jesus Lord, woman." Frank slammed his half-full glass down on a side table. "Hand out guns to the women and watch half the town get shot up from lousy aim." He growled. "Ain't happening."

"How stupid do you think we are, son?" Mama rose to her feet and stared down her nose at both Carter menfolk.

"I was shooting empty bottles and bean tins when you boys were still wetting yourselves."

"I'm not letting any of you take up knifing." Frank waved his arms around for effect, but Vivian could see the worry plain as day on his face. Part of her felt lucky to have brothers who cared so much.

The other part had grown mighty weary of being viewed as somebody's little sister.

Before she could say anything else, Joshua entered the salon. Briefly he met her gaze, his river-dark eyes as intense as always.

Removing his hat, he cleared his throat. "Sorry to intrude, folks. Thought you might want to know, the owner of Gleason's Gambling Galleria just sprang Miss Carter's, er, accoster, out of jail."

Harrison got in Joshua's face and caught hold of his collar in one big fist. "You let him bail out already? The bastard attacked Vivian, not two hours ago!"

Frank crowded in angrily. "What kind of sheriff are you?"

Lord, they'll kill him was all Vivian could think, and she tried to run to Joshua's defense but found herself caught by Catherine's restraining arm. "Let *go*."

"Not on your life," Catherine retorted.

Joshua twisted from Harrison's grip as Frank drew back a fist. Faster than lightning, Joshua caught it in one big hand and pushed it away so hard, Frank stumbled.

"Now," Joshua rasped, "listen here. Mister Gleason came with bail. Until this town hires itself a judge, by law I have to allow one from Silver Cache to come in. You both know that. But I'm telling you once the judge passes sentence, Gleason will have to find himself another worker."

The sheriff's ability to maintain his advantage during this confrontation caused Vivian's heart to flutter, even though she still harbored irritation toward the man and his high-handed ways. Her brothers were big men and could be overwhelming when together. Yet Joshua easily kept them both at bay.

Across the room, the argument grew louder.

"I want to meet this jackass, Gleason," Frank demanded. "Right now. Then I want to punch that worker of his until he bleeds. Might want to punch Gleason too, for bringing this shit to our town in the first place." He scooped up his Stetson and slammed it on his head. "How'd he know one of his men got locked up?"

"The man begged Ben to contact Gleason," Joshua replied. "Said he hadn't meant any harm and apologized all over himself for getting drunk."

Joshua's hair had fallen across his eyes and he shook it back impatiently. Vivian found herself longing to scoop it up by the handfuls, and—

At the very thought, she released a whimper that dropped into a sudden, silent lull. Cringing, she glanced around. Had anyone noticed?

None of her family reacted, thank heaven.

But Joshua's gaze tightened as he swung toward her. By the look on his face, he'd heard her quite well. Heat flooded her from neck to scalp.

Catherine's slender arm tightened around her stomach briefly. "Behave yourself," she whispered in Vivian's ear. "And don't pretend you don't know what I mean."

~ ~ ~

That soft sound vibrated in Joshua's ears and almost took him to his knees.

He had no idea what'd prompted it, except he was aware of Vivian watching him as he dealt with her stubborn, often moronic and consistently overprotective brothers.

He was always aware of her, in any room.

Every time.

Earlier, standing outside the boardinghouse after being interrupted by Nate's mother, they'd resolved nothing. He'd hated seeing Vivian exposed to the likes of Florence Johnson. What that harridan exuded, Joshua didn't want anywhere near Vivian.

After Florence left, he'd wanted to resume trying to reason with her, but Vivian had been too wrought over young Nate. She'd walked away with Robert after the man promised to see her safely to the Stage House and into her mother's capable hands. Any chance Joshua might have had to shake some sense into her was lost.

By the time he'd returned to the jail, a new situation had sucked up a chunk of his time and tied him up in frustration. Turned out Mister Knight Gleason was good at causing uproars. Claiming the soused vagrant in their jail was a woodworker named Doo Spivey who'd been hired on during the casino's final construction and still owed him work, Gleason demanded his release. He'd handed Joshua the man's pay in lieu of bail along with a formal request for a court date. Legally Joshua couldn't ignore either. It burned his gut like acid, but he'd had no choice.

Trying to get that across to the Carter brothers when they were in the throes of righteous fury wasn't easy. Doing it while pretending he didn't notice their sister's feminine allure or smell that flowery cologne she wore like a badge of virginity . . .

Impossible.

Unable to deal with any Carter for another second, and certain Vivian hadn't mentioned Florence Johnson at all, Joshua snapped, "Fair warning. Stay away from the Gleason place. I hear about you causing the man any trouble, I'll take you in. Let me handle things the lawful way."

"I want that bastard run out of town." Frank shook off the hand their mother clamped on his arm. "This is serious, Lang. We got innocent girls to protect in our family. Other families. What if he comes back for Vivian? What if nobody's in earshot when he does?"

"Frank," Lucinda said, "don't be an ass," just as Vivian fumed, "For heaven's sake, I'm not in any danger—"

Joshua pivoted toward Vivian, images of Spivey manhandling her still fresh in his mind. "Really, Miss Carter? Did you share *all* the details about how a drunken stranger walked right into the schoolhouse and put his hands on you?"

It hadn't gone unnoticed to him how she'd wrapped her shawl around her shoulders, crossed in front and tucked in at the ends, the way ladies often did. His anger spiked. Shooting out his arm, he grabbed the back of the shawl and yanked it from her shoulders. Those two smudges lay beneath, showing up on the front of her yellow bodice like double bull's-eyes.

"You—You—" For once, Vivian was rendered speechless.

Frank, Harrison, and their mother all gaped. Catherine slapped a palm over her mouth.

Lucinda was the first to react. "My God—"

The duet of growls from her sons bounced around the elegant dining room louder than a rifle report. Both started toward Vivian, and Joshua wasn't sure if they meant to offer comfort or chastisement.

Regretting his impulsive action, he put himself between her and the rest of her family, fighting to ignore the heat of her body a scant few inches behind him.

He faced her siblings—and mother—squarely. "Vivian didn't do anything, other than her job. But after hours she's still a woman by herself in the schoolhouse. It's my job to protect this town, and I think it's time I hired myself an extra deputy or two. Until I do, Ben'll take on additional hours. And I'll ask around for more help. Best thing you can do is escort your womenfolk where they need to go."

"Sheriff, we're not idiots," Lucinda protested. Her eyes flashed fire, identical to her daughter's when she was mad.

"Not idiots, ma'am. Vulnerable, yes."

Vivian shifted behind him, placing a hand on his back that he felt through his entire body. His heart thudding, he said, "The letter of the law has to be upheld, but I won't allow scum like him to remain in our town. One way or another, he's leaving Little Creede. You have my word."

First, Harrison's stiffness eased, then Frank's knotted shoulders relaxed. Lucinda Carter managed a faint smile, as Catherine tapped a finger against her lip thoughtfully, her gaze locked on him and Vivian.

"Let me do my job," Joshua said. "I'll keep your loved ones safe."

Vivian's hands slid to his hips as she leaned against his back, and for one perfect moment her breasts pushed into his spine. The scent of warm, willing woman teased his nose, and he swallowed back a groan.

She released a barely audible sigh, yet he heard it, and desire swept through him.

It was in that moment Joshua realized he was in big trouble.

Chapter 4

Crowded inside the jailhouse with the judge from Silver Cache, and the entire adult Carter clan, Joshua ground his back teeth together as a visibly uncomfortable Vivian recalled the details of her attack in the schoolroom.

He stood next to Harrison with Frank on his other side. Tension rolled off the Carter brothers, and if it weren't for their women's presence, Joshua was certain the two would be hauling this no-account bastard outside to dance at the end of a noose. Joshua could feel his own fury build, growing hotter with every tentative word that fell from Vivian's lips.

"What happened next?" Judge Wilson asked kindly.

Vivian shifted in her seat, her gaze flying to her brothers before she glanced down at her lap, her hands clasped together. "He covered my mouth and shoved me against the wall."

Joshua ached to pound the scum into the ground. *I'm the law in this town,* he reminded himself. *I can't beat him to death, as much as I want to.*

Her voice quavered as she continued, and he had to lock his knees to remain where he stood. "He, um. He grabbed my, um . . ." Her cheeks brightly flushed and, growing redder each passing second, Vivian touched her chest.

Both of her brothers snarled loudly, but it was Knight Gleason, standing near the door, who reacted outright.

"Why, that scallywag sumbitch." Gleason stomped to the front of the room. "Spivey, heah"—he flung a glare toward the prisoner, who refused to meet anyone's regard—"tol' me it was only a kiss, an' one Miss Carter invited."

"He's a damned liar," Frank shouted, while Harrison lunged for Spivey, only held back by Retta's firm grip on his arm.

Gleason nodded. "I kin see that." He spun his derby in his hands, sending Vivian an apologetic look. "Ah sure am sorry, missy. Ah kin see yer a darlin' gal who'd nevah allow a stranger to take such liberties."

The burly gambler shifted his attention to his worker and any semblance of politeness fell away. Joshua's brows rose at the change in his demeanor. Civility gone, the threat of death stared from the man's eyes. "Ah withdraw mah bail, along with any work ah previously offered this wu'thless skunk."

He turned toward Joshua and the rest of the Carters with a low, sweeping bow. "Ah apologize fer this man's actions, gentlemen, an' leave his fate in yer capable hands."

Frank gave a curt nod of thanks, as Gleason returned to his spot by the door.

"Miss Vivian," the Judge began, "shall I throw this man in jail, pending Territorial Prison incarceration, or order him out of Little Creede, never to come back?"

Vivian studied her attacker, who was at least smart enough not to look her way or Joshua might have forgotten he was the law. He'd have eagerly given the piece of horseshit the beating he deserved.

"I think leaving town and never returning is sufficient punishment," Vivian finally said, far too kindhearted for her own good.

Joshua's knuckles bunched, images of those large palmprints on the front of her gown forever burned in his mind. Then he remembered he'd be the one escorting the bastard out of town. A mean smile curved his lips.

Frank's unamused chuckle drew his attention, and he found both his friends watching him with hard eyes.

"Make sure it hurts, Lang," Harrison muttered, while Frank's jaw flexed.

"Count on it," Joshua promised.

~ ~ ~

When the proceeding inside the jailhouse broke up, Flo scrambled from her perch at the back window, her legs tangling in the fancy gown she wore. She hated wearing all these layers, much preferring the simple clothing that left a woman bare underneath, easily accessible to a man's touch. She wasn't a whore purely out of necessity. She loved men. Though she'd had her share of disgusting miners and cowboys, most of the time she enjoyed her job and the debauchery that came along with it.

No one had been better at debauchery than Slim Morgan. Just thinking of the many ways he used to dominate her in bed left Flo breathless.

Raised voices and shouting dragged her away from dwelling in the past, and she returned her attention to the jailhouse as her mind raced for a way to get what she wanted. With her son's help, she hoped to collect a substantial amount of silver from the mine Slim had stolen off some old miner after his escape from Territorial Prison.

"Mister Gleason," a familiar voice yelled as Joshua Lang tossed him across the back of a horse, hands bound behind his back, "I'm tellin' you the truth. She was askin' for it."

Spivey, you dirt-dumb idiot. Flo pressed back against the rough wall to escape being noticed. Coming into town to collect the fool had been a wasted effort, if he couldn't even manage to stay out of jail. Worthless, just like most men.

She peeked carefully around the corner and saw Harrison Carter grip his brother Frank tightly as he struggled toward Spivey. If looks could kill, the man would be dead. "Hold on, Frank. Let Joshua do his job."

Their sister huddled in the doorway with her hand over her heart, as if one step away from having the vapors. Both Carter women stood protectively on either side of the sniveling bitch. Hate tasted bitter on Flo's tongue. If it weren't for the Carters, Slim would never have gone to prison, losing everything they'd worked so hard for. Plus, Doo was proving himself to be completely inept.

And from the short time she'd been back in town, she'd learned Vivian Carter had a special interest in Nathanial.

With no one available to rely upon but herself, Flo's mind raced to figure out a way to cause as much damage as possible to the Carter family. Something that would draw blood and distract their attention from her.

As the sheriff headed out with Spivey, her focus targeted Little Miss Goody-Goody Schoolteacher Carter. For the first time since returning to Little Creede, Flo formed a satisfied smile.

Yes. I know exactly what to do . . .

~ ~ ~

About five miles outside of town, Joshua dumped Spivey onto the ground. He landed on the dry prairie grass with a hard thump. Staggering to his feet, wrists still tied behind his back, his glare locked on Joshua as he let loose with a mouthful of colorful expletives.

Dismounting Quicksilver, his stallion, Joshua drawled, "I'm not sure that's even physically possible." Striding to the sonofabitch, he withdrew his Bowie from its sheath and Spivey stopped talking, all color draining from his face as he stared at the lethal blade. "But I'm willing to test that theory." He brought the knife—a prized weapon from his Ranger days—to within a few inches of Doo's nose.

The coward backed away. "You can't cut me, you're the law." His panic palpable, he whirled on clumsy feet as if seeking rescue. Only miles of wide-open space surrounded them. Sweat slid down his stubbly cheeks and plopped on his filthy collar. "I dint mean nuthin' by it. If you just let me go, I promise you'll never see me again."

Joshua jerked the bastard forward by his throat, shoving his face close so there'd be no mistaking his meaning. "I'll cut you, all right."

The man started shaking and blubbering, resulting in the first decent smile Joshua had enjoyed all week. "I'll cut you loose," he amended with a growl, "and then you're going to walk out of here." Adjusting his grip to the scruff of Spivey's scrawny neck, Joshua flipped him around and sliced the blade through the rope.

As the pieces fell, a hard shove made Spivey trip over his own boots, though the bastard managed to stay on his feet. Replacing the knife, Joshua got in Spivey's face threateningly. "If I see you anywhere near Little Creede, I can promise you won't be walking out again."

To add more impact to his words, and because he wanted to, he buried his fist in Spivey's gut. When he bent over, groaning, Joshua brought hard knuckles up into his chin, sending him back on his ass. "That's for touching Vivian Carter."

He retrieved a canteen from his saddlebag and tossed it to the ground. "There's enough to last you to the next watering hole, if you hurry."

When the dumb cur just lay there blinking at him, Joshua took a threatening step forward and snarled, "Run."

With a yelp, Spivey grabbed up the canteen and took off, as if his life depended on it. And with those handprints on Vivian's pert breasts still prominent in Joshua's mind, the man wasn't wrong.

Returning to his mount, Joshua swung into the saddle, taking one last look at Spivey's retreating back. While the stallion shifted restlessly beneath him, Joshua held a hand over his eyes against the brightness of the lowering sun, and kept watch until Spivey was a speck in the distance. At least he was running in the right direction.

It'd be dark in a couple hours. If Spivey got lucky, he'd reach Pepper Run before the moon came up. Halfway between Little Creede and the beginning of Rocky Gulch's mine perimeter, the low-lying grasses with its higher weeds would give him a place to shelter. The clear spring water of the run would fill his canteen. If the man was stupid enough not to stop there for the night . . . well, too bad.

Later, Joshua rode into town still mulling over his growing feelings toward his best friends' little sister. Buck Adams sat on his front porch, smoking his pipe and looking sicklier every day.

A dark scowl covered Buck's weathered face. "I hope you pistol whipped that cur for scaring Miss Carter." A cough rattled his lungs. "Anyone who hurts that young woman deserves no less." His rheumy eyes lit on Joshua. "And I do mean anyone, Sheriff."

The warning didn't go unnoticed, and heat crept up the back of Joshua's neck. *The old geezer's far too observant.* "You have a good evening, Buck."

The man's dry chuckle followed him up the street, along with the knowing stares of a handful of townsfolk. Yeah, it'd been a big mistake to allow his frustration toward Vivian's lack of common sense push him into showing feelings that should have never seen the light of day. Now half the busybodies around knew he had a far more than casual interest in Vivian Carter. Wouldn't be long before the other half found out as well.

With a sigh, Joshua dropped Quicksilver's reins over the hitch post in front of the jailhouse and dismounted. Before he could head inside, Knight Gleason, dressed in a suit far too fancy for Little Creede, strode down the walkway.

"Sheriff Lang, just the fella ah wanna see," he called out, his long strides eating up the distance between buildings. "I wanna apologize fer not listenin' to yew afore I bailed that no-account outta yer jailhouse."

Joshua opened his mouth to let the man know there were no hard feelings, but didn't get the chance as Gleason waved his hands in the air and barreled on. "To make up fer mah bad manners, ah wanna do what ah kin to keep mah new home safe."

While the gambler dug in his coat pocket, Joshua again tried to speak. Not fast enough as Gleason continued, "Ah have enough heah, yew should be able to add another buildin' to lock up anyone who dares come to our town an' break the law." He held out a coin bag.

Slowly, Joshua accepted the leather pouch, lifting a surprised brow at the weight. *Probably enough here to add on two new cells, possibly three.* He'd need those extra cells, too, given the popularity he'd already seen for himself of Gleason's Gambling Galleria, and the town's rapid growth.

Again, Joshua opened his mouth to thank the man, when Knight's gaze lit on something a short distance away, spurring him into motion. "Now, if'n yew'll excuse me, Sheriff, ah see a damsel in distress that ah must assist afore she gits that purty gown of hers all filthy."

Joshua turned to see Gleason make a beeline for Hannah Penderson, who was trying to find a way around a large puddle to cross the street. He couldn't hear what was said, but her hand flew up to grip one wide shoulder as Gleason swung her into his arms and plodded through the water, seeming not to notice the mud that splashed his pants.

An unlikely pairing, the gambler and the spinster. But as Joshua watched the two with increasing amusement, he decided they might actually do well as a couple. Gleason set Hannah on her feet, before offering her his arm. Wide-eyed and looking a bit more than smitten, she tentatively took it. He steered her down the street toward The Miner Stage

House with a gentleness Joshua would've never thought possible from such a large, blustering man.

He smothered a grin, turning to look out over the town, noting how dusk had already settled in. Hefting the coin bag, he unlocked the door to his office and stepped inside, crossing to his desk. He'd store the money in a locked drawer until he could get to the bank in the morning.

As Joshua exited the jail, intent on settling himself and his horse for the evening, his thoughts shifted to the lovely dark-haired woman who'd been the cause of several restless evenings. Unable to help himself, he glanced up the street toward the schoolhouse. When he spotted the spark of a match, then lamplight flare inside, his brows snapped down.

"Foolish woman," he rumbled, leaping off the boardwalk and striding down Main Street to the path winding up onto school grounds.

Anger built in his chest at each step. If the thought of touching her didn't make him hard as stone, he'd turn Vivian over his knee and spank her rounded little backside for putting herself at risk.

Again.

And where are her brothers?

After what'd happened, he figured Frank and Harrison would have laid down the law to their far too naive sister.

He shoved the door open so fast, it banged against the inside wall then swung shut behind him as he stomped inside. Vivian screamed, dropping the book she'd been holding. Real fear entered her eyes before she realized who he was.

Annoyance replaced fright, and she slammed her hands on her hips, glaring at him. "Joshua Lang, what is wrong with . . .?" Her voice trailed off as he prowled toward her. She stumbled back, coming up against the wall.

Joshua didn't stop until he reached her, propping his hands on the rough-hewn log beam above her head as he glowered down at her. Their positions only added to his fury, her petite stature even more pronounced. She'd be defenseless against any man bent on harming her.

He stood over her, easily a foot taller, and he didn't miss the awareness that entered her startled gaze. The woman was guileless beyond words. Did she even understand how her feelings for him shone in her eyes whenever she looked at him?

She brought her hands up to his chest as if to ward him off. The gentle rise and fall of her breasts beneath her pretty blouse distracting him, Joshua floundered between anger and desire.

"Are you looking to be molested?" he snarled.

Indignation flashed across her face, and she attempted to shove him away. He didn't budge, bending his head until he could see the dark-gold flare of her pupils, hear the tiny catch in her breath.

Joshua lowered his shoulders another inch, surrounding her. His body tightened in awareness. He wanted to taste her lips, suck the sweetness right off her tongue. Then he'd move to the soft curve of her cheek, her delicate neck as she arched toward him . . . until he reached her breasts—

He should step back and give the woman her space, but he couldn't get his feet to move. Needed to walk away, instead of bringing himself close enough to feel the tip of her tongue when she wet her lips.

The soft moan that escaped her snapped his last sliver of control.

"Ah, hell," he groaned.

Joshua couldn't have stopped himself from kissing her in that moment if her brothers shoved a gun to his head.

Pressing his mouth against hers, he licked at her lips until they parted for him. Bringing his hands down to curl around the back of her head, he slipped his tongue inside, his senses exploding with her heady flavor.

He used his tongue gently, letting her get used to his invasion, knowing it was most likely her first kiss. Then the thought of her acting in this manner with any other man sent a jolt of jealousy up his spine, and he deepened the kiss, wanting her to remember his touch long after this moment.

I've got to stop.

He'd crossed a line that should never have been broached with this innocent beauty. He almost had himself convinced to let her go, when she whimpered again, gripping his shoulders and crowding close. Her tongue tentatively entwined with his, inflaming his need to claim her.

"Sweet," Joshua rasped against her lips. He widened his stance and bent at the knees, wrapping an arm around her slender waist to bring her up the remaining distance, until their bodies touched intimately through their clothing.

The feel of Vivian's lush breasts against him had his heart pounding erratically. He could've kissed her tempting lips forever, the hard throb inside his trousers evidence of his rising desire.

The strong odor of smoke abruptly hit him, and his head jerked up, dragging him from the heavenly recesses of Vivian's mouth, swollen and red from his kisses.

Staring into her darkened gaze, it took far too long for his muddled mind to function. When it did, he cursed himself for putting her in danger as fire spread into the room.

He pushed Vivian toward the door. "Go!"

Chapter 5

Through thick, choking smoke and heat from an encroaching fire, Vivian tried not to panic as Joshua half-carried, half-dragged her to the schoolhouse door, only to discover it engulfed in flames.

He spun them both around. "We'll have to go through the window."

Vivian's mind had ceased to function properly from the moment she'd realized her precious schoolhouse was on fire. Feeling like a rag doll, she allowed him to pull her back across the floor as the rising heat became unbearable.

Over the crackling flames and Joshua's insistent tugging on her arm, came one thought on an endless loop.

I'll die here, with so much left undone. So much unsaid.

Burning tears flooded her eyes until she could barely see, her feet tangling in the hem of her gown. Stumbling, Vivian fell to one knee, crying out at the sharp pain . . . screaming when the pain turned to searing agony. "My leg, oh, God!"

Joshua beat at her clothing with his hat, then his hands, snuffing out the flames which had caught her skirts on fire.

Before she could suck in another breath to vent her fright, he scooped her up and tossed her over his shoulder, then leapt toward the closest window as glass shattered all around them. Her pretty white curtains, now grimy with ash and smoke, fluttered at the edges of her vision as he bore her through the broken frame.

She landed on the hard ground, gagging as dust filled her mouth and nostrils. Someone rolled her through the rough scrub, sharp rocks biting into her exposed flesh, while voices shouted her name. Faces swam into view, Maude and Buck, then Susan. Dub hovered, too.

Why does everyone look so worried?

Abruptly, Joshua yanked at the hem of her skirt, ripping the fabric away.

"Stop," she protested, her weak rasp unrecognizable to her own ears.

"Nate, run and get the doc," Dub commanded.

"Yes, sir." Footsteps stomped away.

Vivian moaned, blinking against the darkness edging her vision. Joshua's face, streaked with soot and sweat, suddenly filled her blurry gaze.

"You're all right now, you're safe," he soothed.

Even as she tried to answer him, to reassure him, smoke clotted in her throat and she turned her head, narrowly missing his shirt as she vomited.

"Goddamn it."

"How'd this happen?"

"Somebody fetch her brothers."

Buzzing commotion surrounded her as she fought for air, humiliated at appearing so helpless. "I'm sorry," she managed, but Joshua only shook his head, a growl rumbling from his chest.

He slid his arms underneath her, careful not to touch the spots on her shins and knees where she'd been hurt the worst, and stood. Cradling her like a babe, he kissed the top of her head. "It's going to be all right, Vivian. I've gotcha."

Gripping his shirt-front, Vivian buried her face against his neck, unable to contain the sobs that shook her as pain radiated through her.

~ ~ ~

She must have fainted, because the next time Vivian opened her eyes, the white walls of Doc Sheaton's office swam into view, along with the lingering smell of his pipe tobacco. A hand held one of hers in a familiar, comforting grip. She blinked hard, glimpsing her mother's tearstained face.

At once, Mama smiled, eyes red-rimmed but steady. "There's my darling," she crooned. "Feeling up to drinking a bit of water?" In her free hand she held a half-filled tumbler.

Vivian nodded, tried to sit up, and fell back onto the examining table, dizzy. Her legs felt oddly pinned down. "What's the matter with—"

"Shh, don't you worry about a thing." Mama set the tumbler aside and helped her into a sitting position, Vivian gasping at the sudden twinge of pain. "Your skirt caught"— her mother's breath hitched—"it caught fire, darling. You have some burns on your legs. Doc says they'll heal just fine, but you must rest and keep them bandaged. Betsey's making you some salve that'll help."

A gruff voice sounded behind her. "Not that black, stinky stuff? She'll smell like a tar bucket." Frank entered her field of vision, his gaze tender. "You're lucky I was at the Stage House when the—" He couldn't seem to finish, and instead swallowed hard, one huge hand cupping her cheek so gently it brought a sting to her eyes.

"I've heard that salve works miracles, Frank." Vivian hastened to reassure her overprotective brother, trying for a bit of levity, not that anything she said would keep him from his anger.

Sure enough, his regard went from caring to furious in an instant. "It can't fix the kind of burns you'd have suffered if Joshua hadn't tore through the wall to carry you out." Abruptly Frank straightened. "Silas got to the schoolhouse first. Said he smelled kerosene." He paced, visibly agitated, while Vivian chewed her lip and watched her brother's fury escalate, the thought uppermost in her mind—

Did someone deliberately set the building on fire?

Pausing at the end of the table, he stared at her with hard eyes. "First it's some degenerate, assaulting you, and now, this." He crossed his arms over his wide chest. "You're not returning to teaching."

The blunt decree put her back up, and she propped herself on both elbows, uncaring the awkward position twisted her bandages. "You can't force me to abandon my students." The retort lost a good deal of power when she had to stop and cough halfway through.

He stomped to her side and hovered over her just as their mother grabbed hold of his shoulder and held him back. "Frank, let your sister be," she began, but her words were lost in the snarl he produced. "Stop being such an ornery ass, son, and stand down." She shoved, knocking him back several inches.

Amusement sprang to life inside Vivian. Their mother was no shrinking violet. Her humor quickly faded when Mama whirled on her. "You can stop your grinning right now, young lady. Your brother might be annoying but he's right about your safety, and you could have been using a salon at the Stage House to do any extra tutoring for Nate."

"I don't want to put anyone out." As an excuse it was weak, and Vivian knew it.

"You're *not* going back," Frank snapped, jerking from their mother's hold. "I'll burn down what's left of the building myself if I need to."

"You wouldn't dare, Franklin Thomas Carter!"

"Maybe he wouldn't, but *I* would." Catherine pushed between Frank and Mama, stepping to Vivian's side, hands slapped on her shapely hips. To look at her you'd never know she'd just given birth to the newest Carter a mere month ago. Dressed in pale green silk and laced inside one of her day corsets, not a hair out of place, Catherine stirred such loving envy inside Vivian, she'd have gone running for the nearest washroom to scrub the lingering soot from her face . . . if she could've moved her legs.

Surely her wonderful sister-by-marriage would take her side. "I must teach, Catherine," she reasoned earnestly. "I can't just quit."

"No one is asking you to quit," Catherine replied firmly, ignoring the low oath Frank emitted. "The smart thing would be for you to recuperate at home, then relocate to the Stage House when you're fully healed and teach there until the schoolhouse is repaired."

"That's not what I'm saying at all," Frank began hotly. When Catherine turned on him, he met her ire with a black frown. "She's too young to teach in a boom town with dangerous types running amuck in the streets."

"Are you implying our sheriff, your best friend, can't properly defend this town?" Vivian bit out, fed up with all the bickering and within an inch of begging for a spoonful of laudanum despite how horrid it'd make her head feel.

And she wanted Joshua to come back in and hold her again.

Chapter 6

Joshua ground-hitched Quicksilver near Harrison's water trough, patting his golden flank as the stallion buried his nose and snuffled. Nearby tasseled grasses, left uncut, would tempt any ground-hitched animal to gladly stay and graze. Retta's thoughtfulness, no doubt.

Blotting his forehead with his sleeve, Joshua stared at the front porch of the tidy ranch. It'd been several months since he'd been out here, and the place looked different.

Then he realized why. Harrison had added a room—maybe two—on the side, where the ground was level and the trees wouldn't be in the way. The logs looked fresh, but in no time they'd weather and blend in with the rest of the exterior.

A sharp, high-pitched screech rent the air, and he grinned as he clomped up the steps and knocked on the partially-open door. Harrison's ranch, filled with children, sparked his amusement as well as a touch of envy. "Anyone home?"

Retta appeared, wiping her hands on a dishcloth. "As if this place is ever empty."

Hair in disarray, a smear of flour on her cheek, the woman didn't look a day older than the first time Joshua met her, several years ago. Fit and trim, nobody'd ever guess she'd borne four children. Unlatching the bottom half of the split door, she waved him in. "The girls are napping with the dog. The twins are currently trying to outsmart their father and avoid napping altogether, little devils. Might as well join the madness."

"Sure I'm not intruding? I wanted to see Vi—er, speak to Harrison if he's here. I can run up to the mine, otherwise."

Stepping over the threshold brought Joshua in view of the parlor . . . and Vivian, reclining on the sofa with a book in one hand and Addie's cat curled up in her lap.

His heart thudded at the sight of her, as lovely and delicate as ever. Then anger clutched his chest, recalling her pain from only a few days earlier. He'd about twisted his brain into a knot trying to figure out how the schoolhouse had caught fire, spilt kerosene or not. Could have been an accident. Could have been deliberate, something much more worrisome in a small town where he knew almost everyone.

If he found someone had deliberately started that fire, regardless of being the law, he might just kill the bastard. Or, at the very least, make him wish for death.

Even as he took a step back, his gaze lingered on Vivian's dark hair, tumbling over one shoulder like a mink-brown waterfall. Eyes downcast, she stroked the little tabby.

"Maybe I should ride over to the mine," he said quietly, thinking to hightail it out of there before she noticed him. Guilt pumped in his blood. How could he face her, after he'd allowed her to be hurt?

Retta took hold of his arm and led him inside. "Sheriff, Harrison's here. I can go get him while you visit with Vivian. She'll be glad to see you." Not one to beat about the bush, it was something he usually admired about Harrison's wife.

Except when it's aimed at me. "Is she feeling better?"

"Her legs have been bothering her some, though she never complains. Well, not until I come at her with the jar of salve, that is." Retta rolled her eyes comically.

"Betsey's homemade stuff? Jesus, the smell alone can dissolve wallpaper paste." Joshua allowed himself to be dragged into the parlor as Vivian glanced up from her book, straight into his eyes.

The longing he spotted in her stare made Joshua catch his breath. Belatedly he remembered to remove his hat, and shook back his hair, noting with a touch of masculine pride how her cheeks flushed a pretty pink.

He stared back, his senses highly aware of the woman he wanted to possess but couldn't have, unable to think of a thing to say that didn't sound suggestive. Thankfully, Harrison emerged from a back room with a rowdy tot under each arm, saving Joshua from making a fool of himself.

"Joshua, didn't expect to see you today." The boys, identical right down to the bone, both shrieked happily, wriggling in their father's grip. Harrison hefted one—Matthew or Thomas, Joshua hadn't a clue which—and nodded toward an empty chair in the parlor. "Come on, sit a spell."

The chair was right across from the sofa, and Vivian, who straightened the soft woolen throw across her legs and attempted to smooth back her hair. From the way the throw draped over the side of the cushion, Joshua suspected she wasn't wearing anything other than her bandages from the waist down.

The desire he'd been unsuccessfully fighting raged out of control as he imagined her half-naked a mere foot away from him. *For Christ's sake, she's injured.* Joshua sucked in a breath, praying his inappropriate thoughts hadn't been obvious to her family.

Lowering his Stetson to groin level, he sank into one of the chairs, hoping to hide his reaction to the highly inappropriate image he couldn't seem to banish from his mind. Meeting Harrison's gaze, then Retta's, Joshua figured he was safe.

He didn't dare look at Vivian as Harrison placed the boys onto a smaller settee, clasping their shirt collars to keep them from squirming away. They fussed then settled, cuddling against the cushions, dark heads together as they yawned and shoved chubby thumbs into their mouths. Blue eyes, identical to Retta's, blinked once, twice, and slowly closed as they fell asleep within moments. Joshua envied the ability to drop off like that. Of late, his nights had been too full of thoughts better left alone . . .

He cleared his throat, remembering what he'd come here for. "I did stop by to see how Miss Carter is feeling"— he nodded briefly toward her—"but also to catch you up on what we've found. Silas smelled kerosene, you probably already know that. It's possible it could've spilled over from the lamp sconce on the front outside wall."

He glanced at Vivian. At her visible worry, he fought against the urge to reach for her. "Until we know for sure how the fire started, you need to be cautious." He narrowed his eyes. "That means not being alone, anywhere."

The petulant pout on her lips only made him want her more, but she was smart enough to remain silent. Good thing, because Joshua's patience was running thin with her continued defiance. He only wanted her safe.

Harrison nodded in agreement. "Exactly what we've been telling her."

Vivian glared at her brother, before returning her regard to Joshua. "It could have been an accident, or maybe that man—"

"We can't be certain it was accidental. And I already checked to see if Spivey followed me back to town. He didn't."

Unable to sit still, Joshua rose and strode to one of the front windows, staring out but not seeing anything except the terror on Vivian's face when she realized their only escape from the schoolhouse was through a glass pane.

Vaguely he heard Retta murmur, "I'll get supper started," as Harrison joined him at the window.

Joshua squashed his goin'-to-Sunday-Sermon-hat between both hands, before he realized he'd all but ruined the expensive white Stetson. "Well, shit." He brushed at the crinkled brim. "Guess I owe myself a new hat."

Harrison snorted softly. "What's that make in the past year? Three replacements?"

"Only one. Millie fixed the last hat I crushed. Your auntie's a gem." Joshua dropped the hat on a side table near the archway leading into the foyer. Peering over his shoulder, he saw Vivian's eyes drooping as she ignored them, back to petting the cat. Joshua gave a silent groan to realize it'd gotten so bad, he was jealous of a stupid animal.

It was time for him to leave, Vivian needed her rest. As much as he wanted to stay and guard her, she had her brothers for that.

By tacit agreement he and Harrison moved to the front door. "I didn't want to say this in front of Vivian," Joshua began, "but the schoolhouse is a complete loss. Might have been something salvageable if not for the kerosene. Couldn't get water there fast enough to save a thing. If the fire was set on purpose, they didn't want anyone making it out alive."

Harrison's gaze swung to his sister, his face blanching whiter with each word out of Joshua's mouth. "At least now Frank won't have to burn the rest of it to the ground to keep Vivian away from there."

Joshua clapped a hand on his friend's shoulder. "I promise, I'm going to protect Vivian. Protect this town. Doing some extra deputizing is my first order of business."

Harrison blew out a noisy breath. "Vivian'll be lucky if Frank doesn't lock her up in the back room and pass meals through a slot in the wall, *after* he's taste-tested every bite to make sure nobody's slipped in any poison."

The Carter brothers were notorious hoverers, to a fault. Something Joshua could understand, because the Carter women were precious and deserved to be cherished. The way he'd like to cherish Vivian, if she were his.

With a final, longing glance over his shoulder toward the parlor to where Vivian now lay sleeping among the pillows, Addie's pup Noodle stretched out on the rug nearby, Joshua scooped up his mangled Stetson, not bothering to slap it on his head. "I'd best get to town and see about that deputizing matter. Keep your sister home while she heals, Harrison. We can find a substitute teacher, I'll ask around. Whoever takes on the job will be teaching over at the Stage House anyway. Silas volunteered to take a list of school supplies over to Silver Cache. Books, chalk and tablets, readers. Whatever a teacher might need. Anything he can't find there, he can put on order."

"Appreciate it," Harrison replied, though by the look on his face, it was apparent he might not be all that thrilled to know Vivian would have what she needed to continue teaching.

Joshua stepped out onto the porch but turned when Harrison cleared his throat. "What?"

"About you and Vivian—"

He raised a staying hand. "There's nothing to worry about. I'm too old for her. I'm too . . . hardened, maybe that's the best word. And I know my place."

Before Harrison could respond, Joshua took the porch steps at a single leap.

Chapter 7

Flo approached the ramshackle cabin Slim Morgan had taken off the dead miner. She snorted, eyeing the crooked structure with disdain.

Why am I even still here?

She'd come back because she had loved Slim Morgan for over ten years, had borne his son, and had thought him lost to her forever. Then, on a dreary day last year when most of her hope of ever collecting ore from the abandoned mine had been reduced to nothing, Doo Spivey knocked on her door in Silver Cache where she'd been renting a small house.

Introducing himself as an impoverished miner working a dried-up ore pit north of Mineral Ridge, Spivey had led her over to a crudely built wagon pulled by a swayback nag. She'd peered inside and gasped at the sight of a broken, barely-conscious Slim Morgan, clearly sitting at death's door.

Spivey claimed to have witnessed a shootout that ended with Slim plunging over the ridge. And admitted he'd scrambled down to the rocky creek bed to see if he could 'save the poor man' but Flo figured he'd mostly wanted to pick a dead man's pockets.

She hadn't much cared to know all the details, because Slim Morgan was alive, and her foolish heart convinced her to take him in and nurse him back to health. Keeping Spivey on as a sometimes helper had also seemed a good idea.

She was coming to regret both decisions.

Slim wasn't the same debonair gambler she'd fallen in love with, and most of her needs now went unfulfilled, while taking care of his. Spivey might have gladly filled Slim's shoes in the bedroom, but she found him repulsive. The only thing keeping her in the godforsaken place was the potential for the rich ore that glittered here and there, promising deeper veins behind the mine's rock walls.

Flo felt her stomach knot with nerves as she arched her back to get the kinks out after the long journey up the ridge. It'd been almost two weeks since she'd gone out to Silver Cache for supplies, and Slim would be angry with her for the delay in returning to him. Not to mention the way his temper would explode when he found out the trouble Spivey, the degenerate moron, had got himself into with his antics in Little Creede.

I need my son. He was just the right size to traverse the narrow passageways of the mine's crumbling walls. Slim sure as hell couldn't go in and she'd be damned if she'd risk getting stuck in there and die from breathing in poisonous air.

As Nathanial's mother, she'd planned to just waltz into town and take him. She'd never expected that twit of a schoolteacher to not only get in her way, but also convince the sheriff to block her from leaving with her own flesh and blood. After the school fire, she'd hoped to get another chance at taking down little Miss Goody-Goody, but the girl had holed up at her ranch and Flo couldn't wait around any longer, needing to get to Silver Cache.

Fury roared through her at the thought of her plans being thwarted, followed by another burst of worry as she contemplated Slim's reaction when she walked in without the boy. He'd been mean before, and though she'd loved his darker side and the acts of degradation he'd forced her to submit to that brought them both so much pleasure, lately there was an edge to him she didn't quite trust. The frequent cruelty in his hard gaze threatened to really hurt her if she crossed him.

Only the knowledge he still hadn't regained even half his full strength, gave her the courage to open the door and step inside.

Flo's heart crashed into her chest when a much healthier version of the man she'd left—only twelve short days earlier—spun toward the door and pinned her with eyes that burned in fury and retribution. His lip curled into a sneer as he barked out, "Where have you been?"

She sucked in a harsh breath when he stalked toward her, anger in every stride, the limp from his bad leg, broken in a couple of places from the fall off Mineral Ridge, noticeably reduced. Scars crisscrossed his face and peeked out from the top of his unbuttoned shirt. They only made him appear deadlier, yet no less appealing. The pox marks on his neck, nearly healed, meant he'd suffered the less deadly version of whore's sores and would survive.

Slim grabbed her by the arm and spun her around, slamming her up against the wall behind her. "I think it's time to teach you a lesson."

Excitement ripped through her as he shoved up her gown with one hand and fumbled at his trousers with the other. Bare underneath her skirts, moisture trickled down her thighs.

It'd been so long.

Flo closed her eyes on a sigh as his large hand circled her throat and held her roughly against the wall, his hot breath on her face.

This was the man she remembered.

~ ~ ~

"Thank you, Mama." Vivian leaned forward excitedly as the wagon came to a stop in front of the Stage House. "I swear, if I had to spend one more day lying around doing nothing, I'd lose my mind."

"As long as you keep your promise, and don't overtax yourself," her mother stressed as she climbed down to tether the horses.

Dust rose off the sunbaked street and the light afternoon breeze did little to dispel the heat as Vivian ungracefully tumbled from the wagon in her haste, grabbing the sideboard to steady herself. Though her legs were healing nicely, her long pantalets brushed against a particularly tender wound on her upper thigh. She stifled the pain, knowing Mama would promptly put her back on the wagon and take her straight home at the first sign of discomfort.

Vivian plastered on a smile as her mother came around the side of the wagon. "I promise I'll be good. Do you think Dub could fetch Nate for me? We really need to catch up on his reading."

Susan and Mark Wilkey had been kind enough to bring Nate to the ranch once for a visit and a lesson, but Vivian had been so tired that day they hadn't accomplished much. Plus, she missed the boy something fierce, and worried about him all the time. Especially with that awful woman back in town trying to get her claws into him.

Vivian couldn't understand it, since Florence Johnson didn't have a maternal bone in her body.

What is she up to? Sudden unease made her queasy. *No good, that's what.*

"Don't look so worried." Mama patted Vivian's cheek. "Dub'll fetch Nate for you."

"Vivian," Catherine called out, lifting her skirts and sprinting down the wide steps of the Stage house to greet them. A smile lit her beautiful face. "It's so good to see you up and about." She rushed over, pulling Vivian into a big hug. "Everyone in town asks about you, and even though I keep reassuring them you're fine, it'll put their minds at rest to see for themselves."

"Especially Buck Adams." Mama chuckled. "The man's been like a growling bear ever since you were hurt. Blames the sheriff for not taking care of you better."

Catherine nodded. "He's mighty fond of you, sister dear. Heck, the whole town is. In the short time you've been here you've captured everyone's heart."

Not everyone. Vivian's temper simmered as the image of Joshua Lang flashed across her mind, even as her heart warmed at the way Little Creede's townsfolk had embraced her. Though she'd only resided in the area a year, this was her home now and she never wanted to live anyplace else. "I'll stop by and visit with Buck, after Nate's lesson."

She'd grown mighty fond of the old gentleman and worried something awful about his health. She'd known others who'd had the same raspy cough, and it never ended well.

Catherine linked her arms with Vivian on one side and Mama on the other as they headed into the lobby. "How are your legs doing?"

Her mother answered for her and saved Vivian from having to tell a fib. "She swears they're all healed up." She shot her a look of exasperation. "But I have my doubts." They entered the main salon where the last of the lunch crowd were enjoying their meals. "She's a lot more like her stubborn brothers than she'll ever admit."

Catherine slapped a hand over her heart and let out a mocking gasp. "Frank, stubborn? Whatever do you mean?"

Vivian snorted, ignoring the twinge in her left shoulder where the fabric rubbed against the tiny spot badly burned from a falling ember before Joshua was able to brush it off. She'd never complain because her family had done nothing but hover over her. She loved them all dearly and didn't want them to worry anymore.

Her thoughts again drifted to Joshua, and fresh irritation assailed her. "I swear, I've never met a more stubborn batch of men than those in Little Creede." She shook her head, frowning. "Is it something in the water?"

Both women gave her a knowing look, but it was Catherine who responded. "A man is only as stubborn as the woman he loves allows him to be." She chucked Vivian under the chin. "Keep that in mind next time you see your sheriff."

"He's not *my sheriff*," Vivian retorted sullenly, following her mother through the dining room toward the parlor where Eleanor Tucker grinned at them from the open French doors. Her love of literature and sunny disposition had made the former saloon girl the best choice for guiding the children's lessons in Vivian's absence.

"Darling, after you've finished your lesson with Nate, you and I need to have a long, overdue talk about the vagaries of men," Mama commented.

"I don't understand."

Behind her Catherine's laugh rang out, sweet and melodic, reminding Vivian of how she used to sing at The Lucky Lady, before she'd bought it from the bank after Slim Morgan was sent to prison. Now she raised that glorious voice in church every Sunday. "What your mother is trying to say is that women have far more control over their men than they realize."

"That's correct," Mama said primly, appearing thoughtful. "I'm sure Catherine and Retta could give you a few good pointers in getting your man."

A hot flush warmed Vivian's cheeks, somewhat scandalized at the thought of chasing after Joshua, and with her mother's blessing. Mama had changed a lot since moving out West. Heck, she practically lived with Dub Blackwood, and didn't seem to give a hoot that everyone knew about it.

Not that I care, as long as she's happy.

Catherine rubbed her shoulder. "Don't look so worried, Viv. This is the Wild, Wild West, and the old rulebook from back East doesn't apply. A woman has more power here. More rights. We don't have to sit idly by when we see something we want."

Excitement raised the fine hairs along Vivian's nape. Could she do it? Could she make Joshua fall in love with her? She worried her bottom lip. She didn't want to force him to care for her, did she?

I just want him to love me because he wants it, too.

As Mama stepped over the parlor's wide threshold, she murmured, "Life's short, darling. Don't let love pass you by. You need to grasp happiness with both hands and hang on."

Catherine nodded. "You see how well it worked out for Retta. Instead of remaining in a town that looked down on her, she risked all and traveled across the country to take a chance with your brother."

Retta and Catherine *had* risked everything to improve their lot in life. Vivian straightened her spine with determination. If they could be so brave, she could too.

"That's my girl," Mama said, while Catherine's eyes gleamed with approval.

They were right, of course. Love was all around her, with both brothers blissfully happy. Not to mention their mother and Dub. Ben and Trudy had found happiness, while the number of years Maude and Buck had been together was surely an inspiration. Though Buck's time on this earth was running short, they'd had over fifty years together.

Vivian wanted the same kind of happiness, and she wanted it with the stubborn sheriff. If she could spend fifty years with Joshua, she'd die a happy woman.

~ ~ ~

"Ben," Joshua called out as he hung the jailhouse keys back on the nail protruding from the wall, "Hank's sleeping it off in the back cell. When he wakes up give him something to eat before releasing him."

"All right, Sheriff," Ben yelled back from behind the jailhouse where he was disposing of the puke-soiled rags from Hank vomiting up three days' worth of whiskey and tobacco chaw.

The old miner lost his wife a few years back to consumption, and he'd been drowning his sorrows in a bottle ever since. If Joshua didn't haul him in once in a while to sober him up and get some food in his stomach, Hank would've already joined his wife in her grave. It was the best he and Ben could do for the ornery curmudgeon, who rebuffed any sort of assistance or sympathy. Hopefully the man's grief would run its course before it killed him.

Sighing, Joshua lifted his face to the warm breeze from the afternoon sun. Images of a particular dark-haired beauty popped into his mind and his gut clenched as he contemplated the devastation a man must feel losing something so precious as a wife, the way Hank had.

Maybe the best plan of action would be to never lose his heart that way.

Too late, a voice whispered in the back of his brain.

Ignoring the inner taunt, Joshua slapped his Stetson on his head and exited the front stoop to make his rounds. With a newly-opened gambling establishment doing a healthy business all day and into the night, trouble broke out more often.

He strode down Main Street, his first planned stop Gleason's Galleria, where a poker tourney had been underway for several days now. Gleason's newfangled idea, something usually seen on a riverboat, had caught on like wildfire and attracted gamblers from as far away as Georgetown. Joshua had anticipated and already broken up two or three fights.

As he passed the Stage House, he recognized Lucinda's wagon and immediately veered toward the eatery. She normally rode her horse, accompanied by Dub, unless she wasn't alone. As far as he knew, Frank and Harrison were still out at the mines, so that only left one person.

Vivian.

He shouldn't want to see her so badly. Should have kept on walking to the Galleria. But he couldn't seem to get his feet moving in the right direction. Instead, he took the four steps to the eatery entrance in two easy strides and pushed open the double doors, entering the lobby. A quick glance into the main dining salon showed empty tables and a few of the hostesses setting tables for the dinner crowd.

Spotting Lucinda and Dub cozied up together at the back bar, drinks in hand, Joshua would've hurried past rather than disturb them or worse, come under scrutiny, but Lucinda looked up and waved.

Removing his hat, he fingered the brim, angry at himself for letting the thought of seeing Vivian rattle him. Last he'd heard, she was healing fine from her injuries. Injuries that were partially his fault, since he'd been too distracted by her pretty mouth fused against his to notice the danger they were in.

He swallowed hard and approached the pair. "Evening, folks."

"Sheriff." Dub gave a nod.

"Hello, Joshua," Lucinda said. "What brings you to our fine establishment?"

Joshua shifted restlessly, then forced himself to stand still. "I noticed your wagon outside."

She lifted a curious brow but didn't say anything.

"I . . . Um. I was wondering if you came alone, or if . . ." Joshua paused. He hadn't felt this level of bumbling since his scrawny youngster days.

"Ahh," Lucinda said knowingly. "You're wondering if Vivian's with me."

He gave up any pretense of making small-talk. "Yes, ma'am."

"She came in to check on her students and met with Nate for a private lesson. Poor thing wore herself out, I'm afraid."

Joshua felt irritation rise swiftly inside him, annoyed at Vivian for pushing herself, but also her mother for allowing her into town when she wasn't completely healed. He opened his mouth to scold the woman, but Dub crowded in behind Lucinda and glared at him in warning.

Taking a moment to get his emotions under control, Joshua asked politely, "Where is she?"

Lucinda spared him a considering look, before answering, "She went to my room for a nap. I'm sure she's up by now if you'd like to go fetch her. Join us for dinner." She stretched, her fancy-heeled boots peeking out from beneath deep blue skirts. "I've been on my feet for hours, so if you wouldn't mind, dear boy."

Joshua had the distinct feeling he was being played. And it'd been a very long time since someone referred to him as a 'boy.' Lips reluctantly twitching, he nodded. The need to see Vivian again and assess for himself the progress of her recovery had him turning and sprinting up the stairs.

"Second room on the left," Lucinda called out in a lilting voice, followed by the sound of Dub's uproarious laughter.

Chapter 8

Vivian stifled a yawn and closed the copy of *Villette* she'd been reading, tossing it on the bedside table. She'd dozed off at least twice while trying to concentrate on the trials and tribulations of Lucy Snowe, Bronte's courageous heroine. Lucy's escapades should have kept Vivian entertained, but instead her life seemed to pale against the novel's rich descriptions of how the feisty Miss Snowe had fared, teaching at an exclusive girls' school.

Not that I'm actually teaching anyone at the moment, drat it.

With a huff of disgust, she folded her arms across her chest and flopped back onto the lace-edged pillows of the bed her mother used when staying at the Stage House. Admitting she still ached, both in body and heart, warred with her need to do *something* worthwhile. She'd thought seeing her students again would help. It only made things worse, especially when two of the girls hugged her tightly and whispered tearfully of how they missed her.

Nate's hug, not as lengthy as the others but certainly as sincere, tore at Vivian's emotions the most. The half-hour Mama had allowed for his lesson was better than nothing, but the boy was so thirsty for knowledge, it had been nearly impossible for Vivian to stop when weariness overtook her. Escorted upstairs by a stern older brother hadn't helped matters, and when Frank unceremoniously scooped her up and carried her the last half-dozen steps, she'd swatted at him.

"Put me down, you big moose. I don't want to take a nap," she'd protested.

Frank had dumped her on Mama's bed, looming over her. "Stay put or I swear I'll turn you over my knee, I don't care how sore you are. Ma says you're to sleep. I see you downstairs again, you'll answer to my right hand." The grouchiness in his rasp had been tempered by worry, so she hadn't stuck her tongue out in childish response until after the door closed behind him.

Unable to concentrate on her book and too wide awake to sleep, Vivian started to climb out of bed, wincing as the dressing gown she'd borrowed from her mother dragged against her injured thigh, when a soft knock had her scrambling back under the covers. "Come in."

Expecting Mama or Frank—or maybe even Catherine with darling little Charity in her arms—Vivian blinked to see Joshua Lang stride through the door, closing it quietly behind him. In one large hand he fisted the rim of his dress Stetson, and all that golden-brown hair of his tumbled over broad shoulders barely contained by the gray-striped shirt and black vest he wore.

A narrowed hazel glare focused on her like arrows on a bull's-eye, and she shrank against her pillows as he knocked knees with the edge of her bed and growled, "You're supposed to be at home, resting. What in seven hells are you doing in town?"

~ ~ ~

Trying to keep calm was difficult enough, but at the hurt in Vivian's eyes, Joshua wanted to kick his own ass for his harsh words. He hadn't meant to snap at her. So fragile and too pale, she huddled under a cotton quilt on the bed Lucinda Carter used when she stayed overnight at the Stage House.

In his mind he could still see Vivian's scorched clothing and the blood on her hair when a shard of broken glass cut her head. How he'd laid her on the ground and rolled her frantically over dirt and grass, smothering the flames as the schoolhouse burned. That image clung like a burr.

If he lived to be a hundred, he doubted the awful memory would ever leave him.

She was too delicate for this town. Too refined for the rough men who swaggered along the sidewalks and toiled in the mines. Didn't matter how good-hearted or hard-working they might be. None of them deserved such a treasure as Vivian Carter.

I don't deserve her, either.

And that bit the hardest, because he wanted her. Wanted to kiss that pouty mouth. Run his tongue down the curve of her jaw. Her slender neck. Bury his face between those pert breasts that tempted him on a daily basis. Until he could tug a rosy nipple into his mouth . . .

Joshua reined in his lust, but had more difficulty battling his temper, realizing he wasn't angry at her so much, but more at himself for not taking the necessary steps to protect her. They still didn't know if the fire had been purposely started, but Joshua had a niggling suspicion it had.

The question was, why?

"Joshua, what are you doing here?" Her soft voice warred with the frown on her face. One hand gripped the quilt covering her legs, tightening and releasing on the cotton. Nerves, no doubt.

Smart girl, because right now he wanted to crawl into that bed with her and take anything she'd be willing to give him.

Stupid idea, Lang.

He sucked in a steadying breath to banish the image of sweaty sheets and twined bodies. "Didn't mean to snap at you, Miss Carter. But you shouldn't be in town." He broke off at her swift inhale, unable to focus on anything but the way her breasts rose under the robe she wore.

She sat up straighter on the bed. "I'm not about to shirk my responsibility to the children. And I feel much better."

She tossed aside the quilt and shifted to the edge of the mattress as if to stand. The wince crossing her face proved she was still in pain.

Stubborn, just like the rest of the Carters.

"Stay put," Joshua barked. "You'll reopen your sores." He reached for her shoulder to hold her still, his thumb sliding against the hollow of her throat. The feel of her satiny skin knocked everything out of his head except for the blazing need to kiss her.

He hastily let go, refusing to look into her eyes, fearing he'd see the same desire that thrummed in his blood, determined to not take advantage of her misplaced infatuation with him. She deserved someone more like Robert, even though the thought of Dub's nephew touching her filled Joshua with a fierce bolt of jealousy he felt to the center of his soul.

She carefully set her bare toes on the floor and stood. Her feminine fragrance hit him like a punch to the gut. As hard as he tried, he couldn't seem to put more than a few inches between them as he reluctantly retreated.

Everything in her, all she was, called to the male predator inside him. Innocence and beauty, intelligence mixed with a womanliness he didn't expect from one so young all struck him at once, and he muttered, "I need to leave."

"I'm not stopping you, but I'd rather you stay." The low admission caressed his ear as Vivian's hands settled on his chest.

Joshua's muscles tightened at her soft, tentative touch. *Shit.* He needed to go before he did something he'd regret, yet he couldn't make his feet move any further. His gaze met hers, and there it was, desire and passion, just as he'd imagined. Vivian wanted him, the same way he wanted her.

God help us both.

The warm room, the womanly smell of her skin, all

knotted up inside him. With another groan, Joshua leaned closer, loving how her pupils flared right before her arms slipped around his neck. His lips brushed hers gently, carefully.

But her hands fisted in his hair, and to his surprise she rose on tiptoe and placed her mouth fully against his. All rational thought deserted him, and he gathered her in until they were joined from chest to hip. Unable to contain the joy of holding Vivian in his arms again, Joshua nibbled at her lips until they opened for him, allowing him inside.

The breathy sound she made jolted through his entire body.

As if trying to get closer, she tugged him forward, the movement sending them back onto the bed. Now sprawled across her, by accident or design, Joshua couldn't resist any longer from taking what she freely offered.

I'm such a bastard, he thought, even as his kiss grew deeper. Desperate to teach her how to respond to him, the promise he'd made to himself, to stay away from his best friends' little sister, disappeared under the heat of his desire.

He tried to ease away, concerned over how badly her injuries must still plague her. She only clasped him closer.

As her tongue curled against his and her murmur of, "Yes," reached his ears, he wondered who'd taken on the role of teacher, and which of them had become the eager student.

~ ~ ~

If this is a dream, Vivian thought hazily, *I don't want to ever awaken.*

Because to feel Joshua Lang, his body hard and urgent against hers on the warm sheets, had been an ache in her heart for so very long. Though she doubted this was what Mama and Catherine meant when they said to reach out and grab happiness, when Joshua had looked at her as if she was his everything, she hadn't wanted to lose the moment. So, she'd kissed him. And thank the Lord, he'd kissed her back.

Vivian understood the basics of what went on between a man and a woman. At least she thought she knew. She'd overheard whispers among the married women in her home town, how intimacy was a messy, painful affair tolerated for the express purpose of getting oneself with child. Yet seeing Mama, so content with Dub . . . There had to be more to the act than pain and, nine months later, a babe.

A new kind of ache bloomed deep inside her as Joshua's lips trailed down the side of her neck. He nudged the edge of her dressing gown from one shoulder. Shivers broke over her skin when his tongue followed the path he'd bared. For endless moments he teased her with kisses that came close to the tops of her breasts, yet he didn't undress her further.

Vivian trembled with a need that she didn't quite understand. But oh, how she wanted him to show her the ways between a man and a woman.

She slid her hands into the silky tangle of his hair, clenching when he would have moved away, his rapid breaths heating her lips. Her heavy lids opened, gazing up into his face as he moved into her view, his expression dark, intense.

One big hand cupped her cheek. "I don't want to hurt you."

"You're not hurting me." Vivian licked her bottom lip and heard him hiss in reaction.

"I don't want to scare you, either." Joshua belied his vow with an open-mouthed kiss that seemed to go on and on, before he eased away and nuzzled her neck.

"Joshua, I'm not scared. Not of you."

His embrace tightened as she arched closer. His beard prickled against skin already sensitized from his touch as he murmured, "You're trembling."

The way he stated the obvious brought a smile to her lips, and she stroked her hand down the length of his hair. "So are you, Sheriff Lang." She met his bold regard with pride that she could affect him the same way he did her.

Yet the glow in his hazel eyes faded as he drew the loosened edges of her dressing gown together, hiding her naked flesh from his burning gaze. "I'm in danger of taking advantage of you, Vivian. I should go. Before we both find ourselves too far gone." Even as he spoke his hands lingered, warm palms stroking just under her breasts. It felt so good, she couldn't bear the thought of such pleasure slipping from her grasp.

"No," she protested, "not yet. Please stay a little longer."

"If I stay I'll make love to you, and you deserve better, honey." He started to sit up, but she clung harder.

"Joshua, please—"

Abruptly the door flew open.

"What in blazes is going on in here?" Frank roared.

~ ~ ~

Ah, hell.

The urge to leap up guiltily fought with Joshua's need to protect the quivering young woman whose mother—and older brother—just barged through the door. Vivian shook in his embrace, and hell if his arms weren't shaky, too.

"It's all right," he murmured, feathering the backs of two fingers down her pale cheek. "I'll explain."

Standing, he calmly faced Lucinda. "Nothing happened, Missus Carter." His gaze slid to his best friend, noting the flexing knuckles and forbidding frown. "Frank, your sister is fine. You know I wouldn't—"

"The *hell* you wouldn't." Frank strode across the room and yanked him outside. Catching one last glimpse of Vivian's despairing face, Joshua summoned a smile for her, then winced as Frank slammed him up against the nearest wall and drew back a fist.

Guess I deserve a beating.

The punch caught him under the chin and rattled his teeth, but Joshua managed to stay on his feet. He gingerly lifted his chin. "Look, Carter, don't you think I know better than to touch your little sister?"

Frank snagged his shoulder and pushed him down the wide hallway. "From what I saw, you touched her plenty, Lang. She's only nineteen, for Christ's sake." He slammed Joshua up against another wall and hauled off with a second punch.

Joshua's head whipped to the side and he saw stars. His cheek stung, but he wouldn't fight back. "I know how old she is," he mumbled through aching teeth, vaguely noting Lucinda striding toward them. Maybe two Lucindas, since his vision had gone blurry. "She's innocent, I swear."

"Not as innocent as she oughta be." Frank grasped the back of his neck and marched him toward the expansive, curving staircase.

Joshua squinted, registering Harrison standing at the bottom.

"Start walking, Lang." With a final shove, Frank sent him halfway down the stairs and Joshua struggled to right himself, clutching the bannister to keep his feet. Both his knees throbbed from whacking hard into the polished mahogany rails.

"What's going on, Frank?" Harrison yelled from the lobby. He gave Joshua a once-over. "What'd you do, Sheriff, pick a fight with my brother's fists?"

Before Joshua could answer, Frank shouted, "Found our lawman in bed with our sister. You figure out the rest, old son."

Harrison surged up the remaining steps in a rush,

looming over Joshua despite being about two inches shorter. "You disrespected Vivian?"

Joshua held out a staying hand. "I can explain—"

He got no further, because Harrison's fist buried itself in his stomach. Joshua doubled over and hit the edge of the bannister, gagging as the force of that blow sent him tumbling down the rest of the stairs, landing at the bottom with a thud and a pained groan. "Damn it, that hurt."

Vivian, her voice fresh with tears, cried, "Stop it. Stop it right now!"

Joshua looked up to see her mother comforting her at the top landing as Harrison stomped down the rest of the stairs. "Gonna hurt a lot worse, Lang, before I'm done with you."

Staggering to his feet, Joshua swayed as Harrison grabbed his arm. He stared blearily around the room. Evening diners clustered here and there, some visible from the main salon, forks halfway to their mouths as they gawked at him. Some had vacated their tables and stood in groups, staring and pointing.

The entire blasted town appeared to be here, eating supper and watching the show unraveling before them. His reputation as a competent sheriff might be shot to shit after this. Not to mention Vivian's reputation.

A loud *harrumph* from the direction of the salon drew Joshua's attention, and he frowned as Reverend Matias slowly rose from the table where he'd been dining with his wife. While she tutted and tried to keep him in his seat, Matias gently disengaged her hand from his coat sleeve and ambled toward the lobby, removing the napkin he'd tucked into his cleric collar.

His nearly-black eyes flicked from Joshua to Harrison, up the staircase to where Frank stood, fuming so hard he nearly vibrated. To Lucinda with her supporting arm around a pale-cheeked Vivian who leaned over the second-floor railing.

Somewhere above, a fretful babe's cry broke the stiff silence, and Joshua saw the burly Reverend smile, slowly.

"Well, Carter family"—he waved an all-encompassing arm—"by the looks of things, we've got ourselves a wedding to plan."

Chapter 9

Joshua stuck a finger under his starched collar to loosen it and locked his knees to keep from fidgeting, as Reverend Matias raised a hand over first his head, then Vivian's.

"I now pronounce you . . ."

Married.

Once the Reverend laid down his decree, Joshua found himself hitched to the young woman at his side faster than anyone could say 'shotgun wedding.'

"You may now kiss the bride," Matias intoned.

The church broke out into applause and shouts of congratulations, except for Harrison and Frank, who'd been staring hot holes of fury at his back. Joshua didn't need to turn around to know both men wanted to lynch him. *And who'd blame them?* He should have never touched Vivian. Now he did what was necessary to save her reputation.

Sweat trickled down the back of his neck from the oppressive heat inside the church, or it could have been the burn of his shame and guilt, that his loss of control had ended with Vivian being forced to marry him.

When Matias gave a subtle tilt of his head toward Vivian, Joshua shifted closer, meeting her hesitant gaze from behind the bridal veil.

His heart thumped hard. On any day, Vivian Carter was beautiful. Today she stole his breath. The delicate ivory gown she wore hinted at the soft curves beneath. The fancy creation unlike anything he'd ever seen at the mercantile or even Silver Cache, Joshua wondered where on earth Lucinda Carter had found it.

My new mother-by-marriage.

Joshua held a great deal of respect for the Carter matriarch. A formidable yet fair-minded woman, surely Lucinda hadn't envisioned her daughter's wedding as a coerced affair to a rough man with an unsavory past. As the son of a whore, he'd been around fast and loose women most of his life. The loss of his own virginity, at the ripe age of fourteen, had been courtesy of two whores who'd fostered him after his own mother was murdered when he wasn't much older than Jenny.

All he knew was quick couplings, raw and dirty. Truth was, he had no business kissing Vivian, let alone marrying her.

Too late.

Regardless of how they got to this point, here they were and there'd be no turning back. They'd work out the rest later, but for now it was up to him to make his new bride feel special on her wedding day.

Knowing the congregation expected a kiss, he slowly raised the wispy veil from her face, and lowered his head. Vivian's breath caught and her eyes got big, right before he brushed a chaste kiss across her mouth.

He didn't miss Frank's low threat. "I'm still gonna kill him."

"Hush, you'll do no such thing." Lucinda's hissing response caused gruff chuckles and feminine titters throughout the church nave.

Joshua lifted his head to stare down at her. "I promise everything's going to be all right."

Vivian studied him for a long moment, and he was relieved to see the worry in her gaze ease. She graced him with a smile as big and wide as her tender heart.

The feeling of protectiveness that roared to life inside him nearly knocked Joshua off his feet. Unbelievably, this beauty was now his wife, and tonight they'd share a marriage bed. His cock flared to life, right there in the church, in front of not only God, but Vivian's family.

Hell, her brothers, too.

He called himself every kind of bastard there was for visualizing Vivian sprawled naked across his bed. Tearing his gaze away from his bride, he cranked his head back to the Reverend. "Are we done here?"

Amusement lit Matias' eyes, as if the man could read every lustful thought in Joshua's mind. "Yes, son. You're free to take your wife home."

Home? The thought of escorting Vivian to his lousy two-room cabin attached to the jail was just the trick he needed to crush any ideas of getting her naked tonight. She deserved so much better. The hard ball in his stomach he'd been able to ignore for most of the ceremony came rushing back, nearly doubling him over.

Forcing a smile he wasn't feeling, Joshua gently clasped Vivian's arm and turned toward the guests. Besides her family, Betsey and Silas had come for the ceremony, along with the doc and his wife. The Washburn brood sat in the third row, lined up from tallest to smallest, and the Wilkeys had thoughtfully brought Nate.

There was no missing Buck Adams' pointed cough from where he sat in the back of the church with his wife, a glare on his grizzled face. The man still blamed Joshua for Vivian's injuries. Not that he was wrong.

I should have taken more care with her.

Robert, who'd been sitting next to Dub and Lucinda in the front pew, stood and stepped forward to shake his hand. "Treat her good, Lang, or I'll have to shoot you."

"Robert," Vivian protested, sounding scandalized.

Robert grinned at her, giving her shoulder—partly bared by the neckline of her gown—a squeeze. "Just jokin', Viv."

Joshua's temper lit possessively at how the man had touched Vivian's soft skin. Robert chuckled and moved away, but his final warning stare said he hadn't been joking at all.

Vivian's family rushed over, her brothers still frowning like guard dogs on either side of Lucinda, who embraced her daughter warmly. Catherine and Retta hovered, chattering excitedly about the upcoming celebration the Stage House staff had put together.

The door suddenly burst open and slammed against the wall as Knight Gleason strolled inside. Vivian brought a hand to her mouth as Joshua gaped at the mountain of a man, dandied-up in—of all things—a dark red velvet cutaway coat and black striped trousers. A fancy rolled Stetson with scarlet stitching perched precariously on top of his mane of wild hair, while the shiny black boots he wore caught the sunlight streaming inside the church windows. A petite woman in a frilly gown stood at his side.

"Sorry we'ah late," Gleason boomed as he strode down the center aisle, one beefy arm wrapped around the woman's waist. "Mah lil' gal heah needed a proper gown fer this shindy, so we stopped by the Mercantile." He tipped his hat toward Aunt Millie. "Hafta say, ma'am, yew do some mighty fine work."

Joshua blinked as Millie Pierce blushed like a schoolgirl. Then his mouth dropped open when he recognized Hannah Penderson, looking as bright and pretty as spring itself. Dressed in a lilac gown with a flowery trim, she beamed at everyone as she clutched Gleason's arm. Joshua would never have imagined the timid spinster could spruce up so well.

Gleason grabbed his hand and enthusiastically pumped it, the force nearly knocking him off balance. "Sheriff, ah wanna congratulate yew and yer sweet bride." He nodded toward Vivian. "Missus Lang, ah sure am fond of a good romance." He released Joshua's hand as everyone stood gawking.

Between the outlandish duds clinging to the Georgia gambler's massive frame, and his loud, boisterous voice, Knight Gleason sucked up all the air in the room. He grinned down at Hannah, winking at her before planting a kiss on the tip of her nose. The woman actually giggled, then flirtatiously batted her eyelashes in response.

Soft murmurs sounded around them, and no small amount of chuckling.

Gleason harrumphed. "In honor of yer nuptials, ah set aside a room fer yer weddin' night at mah Galleria. Best room in the house. Top floor, all the privacy a newly hitched couple needs." The man's grin was as broad as his shoulders. "Stop by the front desk and give 'em yer name, they's expectin' yew."

Joshua started to turn down the offer, until his living quarters behind the jail loomed even larger in his mind. He could not take his new bride there.

Ever.

So instead, he did what any man would do in preparation for his wedding night with the most stunning woman in town. He swallowed his pride and accepted the generous offer. "Thank you, Knight. I appreciate it."

Tomorrow, he'd worry about getting a place to live that Vivian could be proud of.

~ ~ ~

Vivian smoothed the front of her gown as Retta and Catherine chatted on either side of her. What a surprise it'd been when Mama had unearthed the beautiful garment from one of the traveling trunks they'd brought West. A single old daguerreotype photograph of Mama and Papa's wedding day reminded Vivian of how beautiful her mother had looked in the satin and beaded lace confection, with its full skirts and tightly corseted, off-the-shoulder bodice. Vivian only hoped she'd done the dress equal justice.

Catching Joshua staring at her in admiration throughout the day certainly bolstered her confidence.

Mama's whispered, "Be as happy as your papa and me on our wedding day," went a long way toward reassuring Vivian that she was doing the right thing in marrying Joshua, though she still had some deep-seated doubts.

She lifted a hand to touch the elbow-length veil, affixed to a half-garland of seed pearls and knotted ribbons Mama had pinned to her upswept hair. Reliving the moment when Joshua had lifted the gossamer lace to kiss her, Vivian couldn't seem to tear her eyes away from her new husband standing a few yards away, deep in conversation with Dub. The butterflies in her stomach had yet to diminish. From the moment she'd awoken until this very second, the energy in her body kept her strung tighter than a horse thief facing a hangman's noose.

The get-together at the Stage House to celebrate the wedding was winding down. It'd been both a lighthearted *and* stressful event, depending on whether folks were congratulating her on her marriage to the sheriff, or if her brothers persisted in glaring at Joshua and muttering threats in his vicinity. She knew they were threats by the way his eyes hardened each time and the line of his mouth grew tight, though his gaze softened whenever he looked her way.

Such as now.

The affection she read on his face gave her hope he wouldn't resent her for the way they'd been forced into this union. Joshua Lang was unlike any man she'd known back east, larger than life, as if he'd stepped straight out of a dime store novel. He was equal parts strong and tender, Little Creede's protector and champion, and she'd been infatuated with him from the moment she'd first looked into those intense hazel eyes.

I'm not sorry we're married.

No, not sorry, but worried.

With no time to talk about marrying and thus binding themselves to each other, Vivian had no real idea how her new husband felt. Swept up in the planning and execution of a wedding, she'd gone along rather like a marionette dancing at the hands of a puppeteer. And she'd had no clear reason to refuse, since Joshua hadn't balked once. Flooded with sudden guilt at her selfishness, she gnawed at her bottom lip.

Joshua frowned and broke away from the conversation he'd been having with Dub. Vivian couldn't stop staring at him as he crossed the room. She'd never seen him wearing anything other than his lawman's clothes, which consisted of bib-front shirts and dark trousers, paired with the long canvas dusters he favored, concealing the matched set of Colts at his hips.

Today, he wore a somber black morning suit that emphasized his muscled chest and trim waist. He'd forgone carrying a gun, settling for leaning his rifle against the back wall in case of trouble. Not that they expected any, but a sheriff was duty-bound to be prepared at all times. Besides her father and brothers, she'd never known such an honorable man.

Tall and hard-bodied, her husband was extremely handsome, with the grace of a mountain lion as he moved toward her. Mesmerized by the way his hair, lightened by the summer sun, brushed his wide shoulders, Vivian's breath quickened. Joshua Lang had filled her dreams on more than one occasion. The kiss at the church, as nice as it'd been, left her feeling bereft and needing more.

Remembering the way he'd kissed her at the Stage House, right before her mama and Frank came crashing inside, her pulse fluttered with both excitement and anxious trepidation.

Does he even want a wedding night? She hadn't a clue. Like everything else leading up to this moment, it'd all happened so fast.

Joshua came to a halt before her, reaching out to tilt her face toward him. "Something wrong, angel?"

Even as his endearment caught at her heart, Vivian's gaze flickered to his mouth, longing for him to kiss her again. She inhaled softly and licked her lips.

"Shit, woman. You're killin' me."

At his husky tone, she lifted her eyes to his piercing regard. Confused, she murmured, "What? How could I do that?"

He slowly shook his head, his gaze filling with affection. Amusement eased the hard lines bracketing his mouth. "What am I going to do with you?"

His hand, curved under her chin, held a tremor, and Vivian suddenly understood.

Desire.

Feeling brave, she asked teasingly, "What do you want to do with me?"

Raw hunger crossed Joshua's face as he studied her. Unsure of her readiness for what that look revealed, she tensed. Her comprehension of the intimacies between a married couple, as explained by the women in her family, wasn't something she should fear.

That didn't stop the little shiver running through her at the unknown.

She knew her mistake when Joshua's brows dipped into a frown, then his expression smoothed out, becoming unreadable.

~ ~ ~

Joshua wanted to kick himself. *I scared her.*

Admitting it only reinforced the fact that she was too good for him. Too young and pure for the likes of a man who didn't know the first thing about making love to a virtuous woman who deserved kind words and a tender hand.

Not the carnal thoughts her teasing comment created in his mind, of crowding her into the nearest wall and lifting her skirts to finally satisfy the hard edge of lust that been his burden since the moment he'd set eyes on Vivian Carter.

Disgusted with himself, Joshua turned away from his bride, ignoring the ache in his groin as it pulsed like a heartbeat against the placket of his dress trousers. His focus landed on Harrison, who stared back at him as if he wanted to drag Joshua outside and hang him from the tallest tree he could find. Glancing around the room, he found Frank, held back by Catherine's hand on his arm, his warning glower a mirror of his brother's.

I've really messed things up with her family.

The need to flee her brothers' condemning stares slammed into him. His best friends might never forgive him for his actions, but what was done couldn't be reversed. All they could do was make the best of a hasty marriage.

Pivoting, Joshua carefully grasped his bride's elbow. "Time to leave." The words sounded harsher than he'd intended, and he tried to soften his tone with a smile, but it felt more like a baring of teeth.

She paled, chewing on her lip again until it reddened. "Now?"

He nodded, fighting the urge to lean down and let his tongue soothe where she'd bitten herself, as well as offer an apology for being such a bastard. "Yes, now."

"All right." Vivian blew out a breath. "I'll need my overnight valise." She cast about for the leather bag, Joshua spotting it first.

"I'll carry it for you." He retrieved the bag from its hiding place under her chair, slipping its wide strap over his shoulder.

Hoping nobody would notice their departure, he steered her around the cluster of tables. No such luck, of course. It was as if all of Little Creede paused in their drinking, eating, and socializing, to send 'the happy couple' on their way . . .

"Enjoy the weddin' night, lovebirds."

"You two behave, now. Don't break the bed slats."

"I got two bits wagered, it'll be a boy nine months down the road."

Knowing his shy bride would be red-faced from the crude but well-intentioned remarks, Joshua curved his arm around her shoulders and tugged her close to his side, loving the feel of her pressed against him. Her flowery scent filled him with longing as he leaned down to whisper in her ear, "Don't let them rattle you, angel."

As they neared the edge of the bar area, Joshua paused briefly to offer their thanks to Knight Gleason, cozied-up in a corner with Hannah.

He waved away their gratitude. "Y'all enjoy yerselves. Why, those rooms ain't gonna see any use 'til mah family gits heah."

"Family?" Vivian asked, while Joshua subtly tried to lead her out the door, unwilling to drum up any lingering chatter.

Unfortunately, too subtle for Gleason, who formed a wide grin. "Mah darlin' niece, just graduated ladies' academy. Her daddy's bringin' her out fer a visit. Ah expect them next week, heah'bouts."

After a few failed attempts to politely quit the room, Joshua figured he might as well join the conversation. "It's nice to have family around."

"Magnolia's mah dearly departed sister's child." Knight's broad face sobered. "All the family ah got left. Less'n ah git mahself hitched and churn out a few young'uns." He winked at the rosy-cheeked Hannah and gave her a hearty squeeze. "Ah'm anticipatin' mah two girls'll git along like honey on cornpone."

Hannah blushed, and Joshua took advantage of their preoccupation with each other to murmur a vague farewell. After grabbing his rifle, he guided Vivian through the lobby and out the main doors.

Vivian walked silently at his side. A glance at her somber expression verified her tension had returned, despite her enjoyment of chatting with Gleason and Hannah. Anxious to ease her fears, he took her hand and entwined their fingers together. A cool breeze wafted around them as they strolled along. "I know this probably isn't the way you wanted to start a marriage, but I promise to do right by you."

Her unblinking gaze held no guile. "I don't regret our marrying, Joshua." Pink tinged her cheeks. "I am sorry if you feel differently."

Her words said one thing, but that rosy blush only reinforced his determination to take it slowly. "We'll make it work," he promised.

If I can keep my baser instincts under control.

Entering the Gambling Galleria, they passed through the poker tourney, still going on. The players, engulfed in thick cigar smoke and too intent on their game to notice anything else, paid Joshua and Vivian no mind as they stopped by the front desk to retrieve the key.

Vivian wrinkled her nose at the foul smell. "Do you indulge in cigars when you play poker?" she asked as they climbed the grand stairway to the second floor.

Joshua didn't miss the concern in her voice. A lady of barely nineteen had no need of associating with the pastimes of men, their gambling or their fondness for tobacco. Once again he admonished himself for putting her in this position.

Yesterday, she'd been a young woman available to choose any suitor she wanted, including Robert who'd probably never smoked, drank, or gambled more than once in his almost-twenty-one years. Tonight, she was married, on her way to share a bed with a man she barely knew.

A man with dark secrets in his past. Even her brothers were only privy to certain things about him. Joshua's unwillingness to share his past, coupled with his almost-ten-year age difference from Vivian, had a lot to do with why Frank and Harrison didn't want him near their sister.

She'd paused beside him on the landing, expecting an answer. He guided her down the hallway to their room. "Now and then I play poker." He inserted the key and swung open the door. "But I don't like the stink of tobacco."

"I don't, either." Moments stretched out as they paused in the doorway, gazes locked on each other. Uncertain of whether he should make love to Vivian tonight, or try to ease her gently into the idea, Joshua only knew he wanted her.

He didn't like the fact he'd been forced into this union, but nothing changed how he'd longed for her every day for the past year. He never imagined she'd actually be his.

However we started, I can't afford to mess this up.

Harrison and Frank were smart enough to know a man with no past, no matter how upstanding he appeared, would bring ultimate trouble to their family. Nothing unsavory stayed hidden forever. Eventually his time with the Rangers would come up, and with it the things he'd had to do in the line of Ranger duty. He wasn't proud of it, but at the time hadn't been given a choice.

If his new family asked, he'd tell them the truth.

In the meantime . . .

His gaze fell to the beautiful woman he'd married, who stared at him with both desire and a touch of trepidation in her eyes. Everything inside him settled. Solidified. Vivian was the most precious thing he'd ever had in his life. A gentle woman who appeared to want him. Care for him. Believe in him.

He didn't intend to let her go. Not without a fight. If that meant taking on both her brothers, he would.

Mine.

He'd learn how to treat her properly, give her the time and respect she deserved. He'd never treat her like one of the whores he used to bed, this he vowed.

Escorting his new bride into the suite Gleason offered them for the night, Joshua froze, dropping her valise to the floor. "I don't believe what I'm seeing."

But Vivian gasped in wonderment as she studied the room. "It's beautiful." Her anxiety appeared to have eased, at least for the moment. "I've never seen such splendor, even back East at the most high-end establishments."

She turned in a circle and clapped her hands together.

Joshua wasn't feeling the same excitement as he studied the gawdy room, decorated similarly—and depressingly—to not only the whorehouse he'd been raised in, but several of the finer bordellos he'd visited over the years.

Lace drapes were tied back with flouncy red bows that matched the scarlet carpet under their feet. Blood-red wallpaper, decorated with gilded hummingbirds and flowers, stretched over every wall. The furnishings, though expensive, matched the opulence. Fancy sculptures of fat cherubs aiming little bows and arrows at unsuspecting, nude nymphs sprouted from each corner of the ceiling. An ornate chandelier loaded with slender tapers and dripping with crystal teardrops hung above a massive porcelain washing tub boasting lion-claw feet.

An elaborate, oversized, four-poster bed sat in the center of the room, covered by a thick scarlet spread and more decorative pillows than six people could ever need.

Introducing his virgin bride to marital intimacies in this room, in that bed? Joshua recoiled at the thought. If this was the Galleria's finest, he couldn't begin to wonder what the other rooms might look like. Nor could he imagine an academy-educated young lady such as Knight's niece calling a similar room home for any length of time.

"I don't think so," he muttered.

"What's the matter?" Vivian's soft, hesitant voice broke in. Joshua turned abruptly.

In the center of the room she stood, still wearing her bridal gown, an angel surrounded by the trappings of sin. Though in his heart he knew Knight Gleason hadn't intended any such thing when he designed and decorated the room, Joshua couldn't allow Vivian to stay here.

The decadence of the room, against her bright-eyed innocence, only amplified what he knew to be true. Vivian was too virtuous for this place. Too guileless for this rough boom town. And she was damned-well too good for him.

Joshua raked his fingers through his hair and exhaled roughly. None of that mattered now because she was his wife, for better or for worse. He couldn't undo the harm he'd caused because he couldn't keep his hands to himself, soiling her reputation so badly she had no choice but to marry him.

As self-recrimination settled like a lead ball his gut, he considered taking her to the Stage House, remembering how Catherine furnished a few extra rooms with beds. At the very least he should settle his bride in one of those rooms. She'd be comfortable, have family nearby, and he could—

What? Tuck a line of pillows between them in the bed so he wouldn't be tempted to consummate their wedding night? He'd be better off going back to his cabin, tossing restlessly until morning in his lumpy old bed. Because his conviction—that he wasn't ready to claim her—had grown a lot larger since they'd walked into this scarlet den of iniquity.

"I don't think we should stay here. We'll find someplace else," he promised Vivian.

Her smooth forehead creased in a frown. "I don't understand. Why can't we stay here? Mister Gleason kindly offered—"

"No. It's not the right room for you." Joshua cupped her elbow and started for the door, but she tugged against his hold and slipped free.

He struggled for patience as guilt sat like a heavy weight on his shoulders. "I can take you over to the Stage House. Or back to the ranch. I think that's for the best."

"Why would you want to spend the night at Catherine's or the ranch?"

Needing to get her out of that room before he lost his patience, at her, at himself, at the entire damn situation, Joshua locked his jaw and took her arm, guiding her toward the door. "I'm taking you to the Stage House. Then tomorrow I'll escort you back to the ranch, and—"

"I don't think so, Sheriff." She pried his hand off her arm and scuttled toward the bed. "I heard Mama mention she and Dub would be staying in town tonight. I refuse to spend my wedding night two doors down from my family. What's gotten into you?"

"Vivian, don't push me," he warned.

"Oh, I won't." She tossed her head, making the veil dip to one side, and slapped her hands on her hips. "As my mother likes to say, I don't know what kind of bug crawled in your ear and gnawed on your brain. But I think this room is perfect, and I intend to stay."

Chapter 10

The smell woke Vivian first, bringing her out of a jumbled dream where she faced a church filled with family and friends. Wearing only her bridal veil and shimmy, she stood next to Joshua while Reverend Matias droned on and on. Far in the back of the room, Maude Adams hooted and shouted, "Good on ya, missy." Next to her, Joshua held lace drapes tied with scarlet ribbons, and covered her from head to toe—

She sat up in bed with a sneeze, twisted in silky sheets, half-expecting to find frilly curtains instead. Vivian scrubbed her hands over crusty lids, yawning as watery light poured through the windows from the early morning sunrise.

What a stupid dream.

Stifling another sneeze, she glanced around, searching for the source of that awful cigar stench. Maybe it had permeated from the first floor where the poker tourney had no doubt gone on into the wee hours. Her gaze fell on the red and black brocaded fainting couch tucked in the corner of the room . . . and its occupant.

Her new husband, asleep and reeking of cheroot smoke. His discarded cutaway coat and dress Stetson lay on the floor in a heap, emitting additional stale fumes. Scowling, Vivian clapped a hand to her mouth to hold the stink at bay.

I remember now.

Joshua, tight-lipped and angry over her refusal to leave the accommodations Knight Gleason had generously offered them for their wedding night, had strode from the room, the door slamming behind him. The sound of his boots clomping down the hallway had brought her to tears as she wondered where in blazes her wedding night had escaped to.

Waiting for him to return, the minutes stretched into hours, until she finally curled into the sumptuous bedding and cried herself to sleep.

Now as she studied his sleeping form, for an instant she had the urge to retrieve the basin of water from the fancy washstand in the corner and dump it over his head.

Despite her irritation, she snickered. Both Joshua's arms hung off the sides of the dainty piece of furniture, his big feet dangling from one end, his clothing wrinkled, his hair a tangled mess. The couch was meant to hold a petite lady, not a tall, muscled man with the longest legs she'd ever seen.

He'd for sure be sore when he woke up.

"Serves him right," she grumbled, easing out of bed, clutching the sheet around herself.

Finding her valise, Vivian dug through its contents, retrieving the sprigged shirtwaist and dark green walking skirt Mama and Aunt Millie had sewed as part of her trousseau. She shook them out and got dressed, shooting frequent glowers at the snoring Joshua sprawled uncomfortably on the couch. He never stirred.

Uncorseted but presentable, she exited the room, closing the door silently behind her. She'd hightail it to the Stage House and loiter there a while. Joshua would eventually wake and figure out for himself she'd gone to see Catherine and Mama. Vivian huffed, feeling fresh anger.

Fine way to spend a wedding night.

Yet what else could she expect? Regardless of Joshua's caring attention at the reception, he'd obviously changed his mind about claiming her as his wife.

With a heavy heart, she trudged to the landing, trying to figure out a way to make him see her as something other than a child. Taking the stairs, she held up her skirts as she descended.

The first floor was silent as a tomb, not even a ticking clock to be heard. Concentrating on traversing the marble steps without slipping, she nearly ran into a woman climbing up the same side, her hands laden with a tray.

"Oh, I am so—" Vivian blinked once, twice, at the flustered woman, carrying heaped plates filled with a staggering variety of food. "Hannah?"

Cheeks redder than the strawberries mounded atop a stack of hoecakes, the spinster managed a squeaky, "Oh, Lord. I mean, good morning, Miss Vivian. Um, Missus Lang." She'd come to a standstill, offering Vivian an excellent view of flyaway hair mostly out of its customary bun. Her pale brown eyes had a pinkish cast to them, as if she'd been awake most of the night.

Vivian pictured Knight Gleason's proprietary air around the shy woman, and bit back a smile, nodding toward the heavy tray. "That's quite a breakfast collection."

Hannah's face flamed anew. "Oh, um. I was, um, just coming in with something that needed to be signed, you know, and one of the kitchen staff asked me to bring Mister Gleason a breakfast tray, and since, you see, I had to get that signature anyway, I offered to . . ." Her convoluted excuse withered under Vivian's steady gaze. "Well, you know how it is."

"Of course." Vivian stretched out a hand and patted Hannah's shoulder. "Carry on, Miss Hannah, and have a nice day."

Nodding somewhat wildly, Hannah turned and made for the second floor.

"Oh, Hannah?" Vivian called out.

The woman stopped on the wide stair. "Yes, Miss Vivian?"

Vivian tried hard—and mostly succeeded—in keeping the laughter from her voice. "Your dress is on inside out."

~ ~ ~

Slumped over with his head in his hands, Joshua groaned. Every muscle ached. The fancy piece of furniture he'd slept on probably cost Gleason a pretty penny. However, rich folk didn't buy the silly things for comfort, since the cushion under his backside was hard as a rock.

Despite Vivian's efforts to leave quietly, he'd heard the door open and shut. Worried she might vacate the building on her own, he needed to find her, fast. Make sure she was safe. Plus, he owed her a huge apology for being a jackass the night before.

Sunshine poured in through the window overlooking the street. Rising unsteadily to his feet, Joshua dragged himself over and pushed the thin drapes aside, spotting a few horses, a wagon rumbling by, and a trio of giggling children near the mercantile doors. Nothing dangerous jumped out at him. His tense shoulders relaxed a bit as he scrubbed a hand over his mouth and grimaced at the foul taste lingering on his tongue.

Shouldn't have had that second shot of bourbon.

He spied a pitcher and bowl on a marble-topped stand in the corner. A chunk of soap and a bottle of bay rum sat next to a stack of linen cloths. He lifted the soap to his nose and inhaled flowers. Debating which was worse—rinsing his mouth with cologne or belching posies for the rest of the day—Joshua poured water in the bowl and dampened a cloth, then rubbed it inside his mouth and over his teeth.

After dousing his face and drying off, he peered in the half-mirror hanging over the table. A wrinkled, tangled-haired, blurry-eyed mess stared back.

Can't be helped. Impatient to find his bride, he scooped his hat and coat off the carpet and crossed to the door.

A few men loitered about the lobby, but the gaming rooms were closed off, with a posted sign stating the area opened at six in the evening. A dining area, currently dark and deserted, was roped off to the right of the front desk. Figuring Vivian walked to the Stage House, Joshua strode to the wide double doors.

Nobody waylaid him, other than a nod here and there from what little humanity he saw on his trek to Catherine's place. By the time Joshua arrived and pushed through the Stage House doors, sweat trickled down his back from the unseasonably hot sun. Scraping his hair out of his eyes, he headed for the stairs.

"Joshua, wait." The soft voice combined with a firm demand stopped him three paces from the first step. He turned as Lucinda glided out from a side room, impeccable as usual from the tips of her stylish low-heeled slippers to the top of her burnished hair.

Closing the short distance between them, she laid a hand on his arm. "I'd like to talk to you."

He exhaled impatiently, fighting for a semblance of politeness. "Missus Carter, now isn't the best—"

"I insist." She waved him toward the room she'd vacated. "In here, please." When he hesitated, she tugged on his arm. "Now, Joshua."

The steel in her tone didn't bode well for the conversation. Reluctantly, Joshua allowed her to guide him toward a table partially set with linens and dinnerware. Remembering his manners, he pulled out a chair for her. With a murmur of thanks, Lucinda sat, and he chose a seat across the table. At her arched brow, he changed chairs and settled closer.

Enough niceties. He pinned her with a frown. "Is she here?"

"Of course she is, dear boy. Came into the kitchen and grabbed a carafe of coffee and three of Betsey's jam wheels. Grouchy as all-get-out, I might add. Before I could say a word, she ran upstairs. I gave her some time to eat before following her to poke my nose into what I'm sure isn't any business of mine." One finely trimmed brow arched.

Joshua's mouth curved. Vivian's mother knew no boundaries. "I'm sure you made it your business."

Lucinda eyed him intently. "What do you think?"

Joshua leaned an elbow on the table and propped his aching head in one palm. "I think you know exactly what's going on, Missus Carter."

"Lucinda," she corrected. She cleared her throat with a delicate cough. "You smell of nasty cigars and alcohol. I suppose you imbibed in a snort or two last night, after you abandoned your new bride in that tacky Galleria."

He met her stare and nodded gingerly. "One or two bourbons, I'm sorry to say. Believe me, the fumes alone in those downstairs rooms were strong enough to incapacitate me, and cigar smoke makes me ill."

"Joshua—"

"Yes, I left the room Gleason had so thoughtfully provided. Not abandoned." He lifted his face to meet her astute gaze. "It felt wrong, spending our wedding night in a room decorated in red and gold cherubs and naked ladies." At her choking laugh, he amended, "I think it was meant to represent Cupid and his arrows of love."

Lucinda winced. "Worse, I'd think."

"Regardless of how this marriage came about, Vivian deserves her wedding night to be special. That room was most definitely *not* special. When I told her we were coming back to the Stage House, she refused. If I'd stayed, I'd probably have snapped at her, so I left. Spent most of the night down in a gaming room, and the rest on a torture device impersonating a couch." He arched his back, grunting at the residual ache. "Got the sore muscles to prove it."

"Foolish man," she chided. "I'll bring you some coffee and a bite to eat, then I want you to make yourself presentable and go talk to Vivian. She's still upstairs. Probably with Catherine and the babe." Lucinda rose, but he put a hand out to halt her.

"Where's Frank? Am I going to have to knock heads with an angry brother?"

She shrugged. "Frank left to collect Harrison and Richard. Robert too, I think. They went out to Rocky Gulch to check on things." She patted his shoulder. "That should give you some time. Though sooner or later I suppose you'll have to deal with him and Harrison. But for now, you take me up on that offer of food. Get something in your stomach, then go change out of those stinky clothes and come back over. Your bride will be here, I promise."

Just under an hour later, Joshua reentered the Stage House, feeling and—hopefully—smelling much better, his hunger assuaged by a hearty breakfast and wearing clean clothes. Lucinda had fed him hambone hash mounded over eggs and beans. Joshua had eaten enough to last him the rest of the day and evening. He was growing mighty fond of Lucinda.

The thought gave him pause, never having known the real love of a mother. The affection of the whores who'd raised him had been twisted, and even at his young age Joshua had known it was wrong. He forced the memories from his mind. If this marriage had any chance of sticking, he couldn't let memories of his prior life intrude.

Removing his hat, he started up the curving staircase, this time determined to speak to his wife before anyone else could interrupt. A few steps from the half-landing, a soft coo brought him to a stop, and Joshua looked up. Right into Vivian's eyes.

His breath snagged in his lungs.

In the late morning light she glowed, her hair a dark shiny ribbon over one shoulder, her skin flushed a soft pink. The youngest Carter, month-old Charity, lay asleep on her other shoulder. The sight of his wife cradling an infant tugged at Joshua like nothing he'd ever felt. The beautiful, innocent image they made would remain in his mind forever. In that second, he knew the secret to happiness in this life would be Vivian Carter with his babe in her arms.

He struggled to find his voice but had to clear his throat and try again. Her accusing stare never left his as she rocked Charity. Finally, Joshua got out a careful, "Vivian, I'm sorry."

The single tear that brimmed, then rolled down her cheek, felt like a mule kick to the gut. "Me, too," she whispered.

Joshua advanced, until he stood on the step right below hers. He brought his thumb to her cheek and wiped away the moisture. Encouraged by the way she leaned slightly into his touch, he nodded toward the sleeping child. "She looks good in your arms."

"I love her so much already." Vivian snuggled Charity close and dropped a kiss atop her wispy reddish locks. "Someday I'd like to have—" She broke off, a flush coloring her face.

"Have what?" Joshua teased.

One step higher put him on the half-landing with his blushing bride. He curled an arm around her, encompassing Charity as well. "You can tell me, angel."

"Children," came Vivian's low reply. She didn't pull away, but her slender shoulders tensed a bit. "A child is a part of being contentedly married." She eyed him narrowly. "Don't you think?"

With a look and a few words, she'd neatly cornered him, and Joshua knew it. What could he say that wouldn't start an argument, or worse, drive her away?

Better to change the subject completely. He urged her forward a step. "Why don't I take you home?"

She wouldn't budge off the landing. "Whose home?"

He sighed, not looking forward to the conversation sure to follow. "Not mine, Vivian. It isn't fit for a lady, please trust me on that."

Backing away, she leaned against the dividing wall, tenderly jouncing her niece when she started to awaken and fuss. "Shouldn't I be the judge of what's fit for me?"

"I don't want you living in a two-room hovel behind a jailhouse, Missus Lang." Joshua reached for her, but she inched further away. "Vivian, please. Let me take you to your ranch where you'll be comfortable while I find a decent place for us to live—"

"What did you do now, Lang?" a gruff voice echoed from above.

Rolling his eyes irritably, Joshua looked over his shoulder. Frank stood near the railing, big hands clasping the polished wood hard enough to leave dents behind. His brows formed a straight line over a fulminating stare. Beside him, Catherine offered a resigned smile, tempered with a wink Joshua felt certain that, if seen by her husband, would anger him even more.

Against his better judgement his lips twitched in amused response.

"You think this is funny?" Frank growled. "My little sister runs here first thing after her wedding night, all upset, won't talk to anyone." He made for the stairs, ignoring his wife's staying hand.

"I didn't do a damn thing, Carter." Joshua stood his ground. He was done being accommodating to his wife's brothers and their fists.

Unexpectedly, Lucinda stepped between them. "Stop it right now. You"—she turned to her fuming son—"are acting like a buffoon in front of your wife and daughter." She lifted Charity from Vivian's arms and handed her over, leaving Frank with no choice but to clutch the babe with both hands. "Here, make yourself useful."

He cuddled his daughter into one arm. "The *hell*, Ma—"

"Don't cuss in front of our child," Catherine chastised. She grabbed his free arm and dragged him away. "None of this is our concern."

Joshua's growing admiration for the new women in his life got a fast reduction when Lucinda spun to him, a finger pointed at his chest.

"And you." She drilled into his shoulder. "You left your bride alone. Doesn't matter why. But I know you're going to apologize and then make it up to her. Aren't you?"

"Of course. As soon as I find us a decent place to live," Joshua promised.

"Well, then, isn't it handy that I know the perfect place?" Lucinda crossed her arms decisively. "You'll live at the ranch."

Both he and Vivian gaped in unison.

"What?" Vivian got her voice back first. "Mama, we can't live at the ranch with you." At her mother's raised brows, she amended, "Only because you have company. I mean—oh, you know what I mean. And we can't live with Harrison and Retta. My goodness, it would be a catastrophe." She eyed Joshua irritably. "I don't see why we can't live in your lodgings behind the jail."

"No," Joshua retorted firmly. "Absolutely not."

"Darling, you know I am so rarely out there anymore." Lucinda settled a placating hand on her daughter's flushed cheek. "If you and Joshua don't use that very comfortable ranch house your brothers so thoughtfully built for us, it'll just go to waste and become a haven for vermin and spiders."

At Vivian's shudder, she pressed, "It's close enough to Harrison and Frank's ranches that they cannot complain about lack of safety. Dub's nephews use it sometimes, but I doubt it matters to them where they live. Since Dub's in town with me all the time anyway, they could bunk in his cabin out by the mine."

The woman said it matter-of-factly, without a single blush for what amounted to living in sin with a man. Joshua admired that about her.

She caught hold of Vivian's hand and squeezed, shaking it to and fro a few times. "It's a good place for you and Joshua. You'll have security, it's quiet, roomy, perfect for a newly married couple."

"But I want to live in town," Vivian protested. She whirled to face Joshua, her mouth pinched. "I need to be closer to my students, to Nate."

He gazed at her, seeing how disappointment etched her pretty features like sand scratching glass. Though he longed to give her everything she asked from life, what she needed the most right now was a man who would treasure her, be worthy of her, protect her.

Of course she yearned for the town life. Joshua couldn't blame her. Smart, loving, kind . . . wanting so badly to teach, to guide.

Wanting a family of her own.

Not knowing for certain how the schoolhouse caught on fire, the nagging feeling it had been set on purpose still lingered in his mind. If someone wanted her hurt, she wouldn't be safe until they were caught.

In contrast, the ranches were protected day and night. Lucinda's ranch also boasted two bedrooms.

Two.

He could keep her safe. From anyone who'd do her harm—including himself if necessary.

Slowly he turned to Lucinda and nodded. "Thank you for the offer. We'll take you up on it. For now."

Chapter 11

Flo dismounted at the edge of town, tossing the horse's reins over a low bush. Today, she'd dressed in a cheap cotton dress similar to what the miner's wives wore, her hair tucked under a faded bonnet with a wide brim. Hopefully, she could sneak into town and grab her son without anyone noticing.

If she returned without Nathanial this time, Slim might actually hurt her. A chill ran through her at the thought. She liked a bit of pain, but she wasn't sure the man wouldn't take it too far if he was angry enough.

I need to get that silver out of the mine, before Slim has no use for me again.

Their relationship had been a rocky one, and he'd abandoned her on more than one occasion over the years.

But he always comes back.

Yet her infatuation with him was waning. The tumble off Mineral Ridge and subsequent pounding his body had taken on the rocks along the whirling rapids of Higher Bonney Creek had broken more than ribs and limbs. His mind seemed affected, too. He wasn't the same man she remembered. Oh, he'd always had a cruel side, but there'd been a part of him that could show kindness when it suited him. There was no kindness remaining in Slim Morgan today. Just pure cunning and brute force, his sanity questionable.

That knowledge made it more imperative that she not fail.

Flo strolled along Main Street, keeping her head tilted down to shield her face, determined the sheriff wouldn't stop her. This time of day she ought to run across Nathaniel returning home from school. The last time she'd snuck into town, she'd overheard a conversation between a couple of old biddies. That nosy schoolteacher was back to teaching, this time using a room at the former Lucky Lady Saloon.

Too bad the fire didn't kill her dead when the schoolhouse burned to the ground.

"Next time I'll use more kerosene," Flo muttered, walking faster.

When a wagon approached, she hastily retrieved her hanky from her reticule to cover her face, as dust stung her eyes and tickled her nose. How she hated being back in this godforsaken town, with its lack of modernization or the conveniences offered by Silver Cache.

The sooner she could return home, the happier she'd be. Her gaze searched for Nathanial as she approached the mercantile. She should be able to snatch the brat as he crossed the alley behind the milliners, the fastest route to the edge of town where a few small cabins sat clustered together.

Her upper lip curled as she neared the back trail leading to the former saloon. *The Miner Stage House.* What a stupid name. Knowing that slut Cat Purdue owned it still riled her up.

Spying her son, she hurried into the alleyway, blocking his path. The blankness in his eyes when they met hers affirmed that he didn't recognize her at all. Her temper instantly boiled up as instinct took over. Flo raised her hand and slapped him, like she'd done many times before.

The look of shock in his eyes helped calm her emotions, and she sneered down at him. "Miss me, son?"

When Nathanial finally realized who she was, the expression that crossed his face, almost identical to his father's when he was angry, had her taking a hasty step back. He'd grown since she'd left town for a better life after Slim's arrest. Now his head nearly reached her shoulder. At the young age of nine—or was it ten?—the boy showed signs of the man he'd be someday.

But he's still just a child.

Shaking off her hesitation, she grabbed his arm. "You're coming with me."

Nathanial's thick brows snapped together, and he jerked away from her. His hands balled into fists at his sides. "I'm not going anywhere with you."

At the sudden, deeper edge to his voice, Flo's belly twisted with unease. Before she could reassert herself and force him, he turned and dashed down the alley, disappearing around the corner.

Well, shit. That hadn't gone how she'd expected it to at all. The boy she remembered had been compliant, easy to manage, and obeyed her every order. He knew he'd get his ass beat if he didn't.

How could he have changed so drastically in only a year? And more importantly, how was she supposed to get him to leave with her? The anxiety she'd been able to tamp down so far erupted like a molten volcano, taking her breath and burning her chest.

Slim really was going to kill her.

~ ~ ~

"Is that all you've got?" Frank growled, eyeing the canvas haversack tossed over Joshua's shoulder as he exited the jailhouse.

"It's all I'm gonna need," Joshua replied. The sack was a leftover memento from his Ranger days, and he'd jammed it with enough to get him through a week. He shot both Frank and Harrison an irritated glower, knowing they'd insisted on riding out with him to the ranch so they could have a little *discussion* along the way.

Meanwhile, Vivian was at the ranch helping Lucinda and Dub pack up the rest of her belongings. His mother-by-marriage planned on moving into the Stage House indefinitely. "I don't figure on being at your mother's place for long, just until we find out the truth behind the fire. I'm still half-convinced it was set on purpose."

Joshua flung the sack across his saddle and secured it. "Once her safety is no longer an issue, I'll find accommodations for us closer to town. Not only for Vivian's teaching, but because I need to be here when trouble happens."

"You *need* to take care of my sister, Lang," Frank said gruffly, "and let us worry about the town." He nodded toward Harrison. "We already talked with Ben and Dub, and they'll cover things in your absence."

Joshua opened his mouth to protest but snapped it shut, swallowing his frustration. He couldn't stay at the ranch to protect his wife, and also protect his town.

"Dub's nephews volunteered to help out when needed," Harrison added flatly. "So you concentrate on taking care of Vivian, and don't worry about Little Creede."

Joshua gave his haversack one final tug, then slowly turned to face both Carter brothers. They watched him with identical hostile expressions. Thumbing back his Stetson, he squinted against the bright sun dipping in the sky toward evening. "Listen, I know my marriage to Vivian started off all wrong, but I intend to make it right."

"Is that so?" Frank drawled skeptically.

"Yeah. And I'd appreciate it if you two would get off my ass."

Harrison stepped forward in a threatening manner at the same time Frank retorted, "Wrong answer, Lang."

Joshua shifted, muscles tight as he braced for battle. Maybe a good fistfight would help clear the air between them. He bared his teeth and waved them over with one hand. "Do your best, boys."

They all froze at the sound of Nate hollering for Joshua. In unison, they turned to see the boy tearing up the middle of Main Street as if being chased by the devil himself.

"What is it?" Joshua asked, when Nate came to a stumbling halt in front of him. He cupped the back of the boy's head in a gesture of comfort. It was evident something had spooked him bad. "What happened?"

Nate gulped, and Joshua could see him struggling with his fears. Nate won, resolutely squaring his shoulders. "My ma, she's here and tried to get me to go with her." His upper lip curved into a snarl. "I'm never going back."

Pride swamped Joshua at the boy's toughness. He might be young, but Nate was more courageous than most full-grown men. Only last year he'd thrown himself in front of a bullet meant for Vivian, possibly saving her life.

Joshua knelt and tugged him into his arms. Nate came willingly, tucking his head into Joshua's chest. "I promise, you'll never have to go anywhere with her."

Nate lifted his face to Joshua's steady regard with a resigned look in his eyes far too adult for his tender age. "The Wilkeys can't keep me. They're good people, but they're all tied up with the new young'un." He shrugged. "They hardly even know I'm there. What's to stop her?"

As a wave of affection threatened to overwhelm him, Joshua's heart broke a little for all Nate had endured already in his short life.

That woman'll never get her claws into this brave boy.

He couldn't figure out why she even wanted Nate, but it sure wasn't for anything good. "I'll stop her. You're coming home with me."

The words popped out of Joshua's mouth without a thought. It only took a second for him to realize he didn't regret them. Not one damn bit. Vivian loved Nate, and she'd be thrilled to take him in. Maybe they could even adopt him someday.

If I can do right by my wife and make this marriage work.

"Really?" The hope in the boy's eyes loosened the last sliver of doubt in Joshua's gut.

"You bet, little partner." Joshua got to his feet. "How about it? Wanna come live with me and Missus Vivian?"

Nate nodded eagerly, a wide grin spreading across his face. "Yes, oh yes." He threw his arms around Joshua's waist and hugged him tightly.

Emotion clogged his throat as he returned the boy's embrace, blinking moisture from his eyes.

A heavy palm landed on his shoulder and he glanced up into Harrison's approving gaze. "That's a good step in making my sister happy, Lang."

"Yeah," Frank grumbled, amusement plain in his voice. "Guess we don't have to kill you after all." He chuckled, and slapped Joshua on the back a bit harder than necessary. "Let's go gather Nate's things, and head on out to the ranch."

~ ~ ~

"Mama," Vivian called from the parlor, "did you want to take the family Bible along with you?" The heavy tome was an heirloom, handed down through several generations. As an only child, Mama had received it from her own mother when Vivian was quite young. Mama read a passage out loud every night before retiring to bed.

"You keep it, darling," her mama yelled. "You'll soon have a child of your own to read to."

Heat warmed Vivian's cheeks at the thought of being with Joshua in a way that would get her with child. It was both terrifying and exciting. Mostly exciting . . .

"It'll never happen if he refuses to touch me," she muttered to herself, replacing the Bible on the shelf with a bit too much force. Vivian had spent the last few days at the ranch helping Mama and Dub pack the wagon with her mother's belongings, while Joshua stayed at the jailhouse.

She huffed in disgust. A wife for almost a week already, and she'd yet to spend a night with her husband.

She couldn't contain a smile when her mama's voice hissed in exasperation, "Dub Blackwood, if you ask me to marry you one more time—"

Her words were cut off when Dub rumbled, "C'mere, darlin', let me show you all the reasons why you belong with me."

Mama's giggle was followed by the sounds of smooching, and Vivian rolled her eyes. The two carried on like a newly hitched couple, and she didn't understand her mother's reticence about accepting the man's proposal. They were perfect together.

She worried her bottom lip, feeling hurt that her husband didn't treat her with the same attention. Maybe it'd been a mistake to marry Joshua, seeing as he'd been forced into this union. Even though he dealt with her kindly, Vivian had to wonder if he'd leave her at the first opportunity. Divorces were easier to obtain these days, yet they were still highly discouraged by the church and very expensive. She supposed he could just abandon her.

Joshua would never do that. He's too honorable.

Tears pricked her eyes. Did she want to spend the rest of her life with a man who only stayed with her out of obligation?

At the sound of approaching horses, Vivian moved to the window, pulling back the white lace curtains to peer outside. Her brows shot up at the sight of Joshua approaching with Frank and Harrison, then she gasped aloud to see Nate as well. The boy rode behind her husband, but even in the waning late-afternoon light there was no missing the huge grin on his face as he peered around Joshua's back and stared at the ranch house.

What in heavens is going on?

Dropping the curtain back into place, Vivian hurried outside to meet them. Mama and Dub were already on the porch.

"Looks like your husband brought Nate for a visit." Mama gently elbowed Vivian in the side. "Isn't that so thoughtful of him?"

Vivian nodded as Joshua came to a halt a few feet from where they stood. He sought her out with a tentative smile as he swung Nate down from the saddle.

The child's grin widened, if that was even possible, but he didn't approach her. Her husband and brothers silently dismounted.

"Hello, Nate," she said warmly.

He shuffled in place, appearing nervous. "Hi, Missus Vivian."

Joshua and Harrison retrieved a few bulky sacks off their horses.

Joshua's things?

Her husband approached, ruffling the top of Nate's head and nudging him forward on the way. They stepped onto the front porch together, and she got the feeling something big was happening. The anticipation she sensed matched the brightness shining from Nate's eyes.

Glancing back at her brothers, she noticed they were both watching the interaction with a steady concentration.

"Angel," Joshua said hesitantly, "Nate had a bit of trouble in town."

Her gaze flew to the little boy, and she instinctively reached for him. "What kind of trouble?" She didn't miss the way Nate leaned into her embrace.

"Florence waylaid him in the alley behind the mercantile and tried to force him to leave with her." The words were spoken softly, but Joshua's anger rang through.

Vivian's arms tightened around Nate, the fierce need to keep him safe welling up inside her, while her mother cussed under her breath.

Ready to let fly with some choice oaths of her own, Vivian's ire calmed when she looked up at her husband and spied the smile curving his mouth. He tucked a stray strand of hair behind her ear. "Nate's going to be staying with us for a while. If that's all right with you."

The rightness of those words held a settling effect and she nodded, the affection she held for her husband growing stronger. Joshua Lang was a good man who'd spent his days protecting others, first as the sheriff to Little Creede, then as a gentleman who married her to safeguard her reputation. Now he'd become a hero to this young boy they both cared for so much.

Her doubts about their marriage fell away.

"Can I stay, Missus Vivian?" Nate asked, staring up at her, those big dark eyes filled with uncertainty.

As if she'd ever say no. She loved the child as if he were hers, and in that instant Vivian knew she'd never let him go. Her heart filled to bursting with happiness, she bent to press a kiss to Nate's forehead. "Of course, darling. It's the best wedding present ever."

Her brothers approached, Harrison murmuring, "Good man," as he passed.

Frank slapped Joshua on the back with enough force to push him forward an inch, and grunted, "Maybe you're not such an ass," before he too entered the house.

"I wish he'd stop doing that," Joshua growled under his breath, but loud enough to hear.

Mama laughed, taking Nate's hand. "C'mon, young man. Let's get you settled into your room, and you can help with dinner."

Nate's boyish giggle, filled with happiness and unlike any laugh Vivian had ever heard from him, filled the air and made the world brighter. As he left with her mother and Dub, Vivian stared into her husband's eyes, knowing her emotions would be clear to read. "Thank you."

"Welcome, angel." He leaned in for a tender kiss and murmured against her lips, "We'll keep him."

Chapter 12

Vivian sank onto the sofa, stifling a yawn. "Nate's asleep." She slipped out of her shoes, too weary herself to bother with the niceties. When she caught Joshua's amused appraisal from the adjoining chair, she figured he wasn't offended by her stocking-clad toes.

He set aside the book he'd been riffling through. "Where'd you put him?"

"My room. I moved some of my things from the wardrobe to make a spot for his shirts and trousers." She unpinned her hair, sighing at the instant relief. "He's going to need new shoes very soon. Probably some shirts as well." She fussed with her heavy locks, bending her head to ease the stiffness at her nape. "I can turn the hems on a few pairs of trousers but the rest need replacing."

At Joshua's sharp inhale, she glanced up, one hand still tangled in her curls, and frowned at the strained expression he wore. "What is it? If that's too much money to spare right now, I can get Aunt Millie to help me patch—"

"No." His low voice vibrated in the air. "Money isn't an issue." His penetrating stare locked on her. "I like it when you wear your hair down." His tone thickened and dropped even more. "It's very lovely."

"Oh." Heat suffused her cheeks. He hadn't moved, yet it felt as if he'd touched every inch of her.

Settle yourself, simpleton.

Other than a soft touch of his lips to hers earlier in the day, Joshua hadn't come near her except to hold out her chair at supper. Under Nate's curious eyes and in the presence of both Mama and Dub, polite conversation had ruled around the table, offset by the occasional wink Dub sent Mama's way. One of those winks resulted in Mama blowing Dub a kiss. Though a mite intimate for a young boy to witness, Vivian thought the gesture endearing.

I'm envious of my own mother. The notion was disquieting to say the least.

Joshua rose from the chair and stepped across the room, holding out a hand. "Shall we retire? I think we both need a good night's sleep."

"In the same bed?" The words popped out before she could stifle them.

He froze, nostrils flaring, before he cupped her elbow. "I can sleep on the sofa, Vivian."

Striving to keep her nerves steady and her blushes under control, she allowed him to pull her to her feet. Swallowing, Vivian faced her husband. "Mama's bed is, um, large. There's plenty of room for, you know, both of us."

The tenderness in his eyes nearly undid her. "If you're certain."

"I . . ." Sucking in a breath, she ordered her heart to behave. "Yes. I'm certain."

~ ~ ~

Whimpers and a choking sob awoke her. Vivian bolted upright, disoriented and struggling to pry open her eyes.

On the other side of the bed, Joshua hadn't stirred. Surprising, since she'd have thought lawmen were light sleepers owing to their dangerous occupation.

Another whimper, this one pitifully distressed.

Nate. The poor child was no doubt plagued with bad dreams. Rising, Vivian donned the robe she'd left at the foot of the bed and crossed to the door, silently berating Florence Johnson for her cruelty.

She hurried down the short hallway to her old room, pushing at the half-open door. In the dimness of a lit wall sconce, Nate huddled in the middle of twisted bed linens with his face pressed against his knees, his narrow shoulders shaking.

"Oh, darling." Her mother's favorite endearment came easily to Vivian's lips as she sat next to Nate and slipped her arms around him, drawing him close. With a shudder, he curled into her embrace. "It's all right," she crooned softly. "It's just a bad dream."

"I can't—can't . . . it's so dark." Nate's thin frame trembled.

Vivian brushed sweat-dampened hair out of his eyes. "Dark where?"

Not answering, he burrowed deeper into her shoulder.

"Nate?" Vivian rubbed his back, hoping her ministrations soothed him at least a little.

"Don't lock me in there again."

"Where?"

Seconds stretched into almost a minute before he mumbled, "Closet."

"Oh, no." She rocked him gently, stroking his tangled curls, until he fell back asleep. Easing away, Vivian studied the small face, tear tracks drying on slightly grubby cheeks. Her heart melted anew at how beautiful the boy was, how hard he tried to be tough, yet how fragile he seemed right this moment.

"You're mine," she whispered, laying him carefully against the pillows and covering him with the rumpled blanket he'd kicked off. "I'll never let anyone hurt you, ever again."

"What's going on?" Joshua stood in the doorway, knuckling his eyes, bare-chested and clad in a pair of linen smalls that didn't leave much to the imagination.

Her cheeks flamed as she stood. "Nate had a bad dream."

She gently pushed Joshua from the room with both hands, fighting to ignore the muscled feel of his chest beneath her palms.

Once inside their bedroom, he grasped her elbow and guided her toward the bed. "Sit down, you look exhausted."

Vivian settled with a troubled sigh. "I don't think he woke up at all, though he looked right at me. He said it was dark, begged not to be locked in the closet again, and then he just closed his eyes. He'd been crying."

Joshua scrubbed his hand across his stubbled jaw. "What kind of monster locks a kid in a closet?"

"I know. He's been through a lot, Joshua. Eventually we'll need to get him to talk to us." She stifled a yawn. "What time is it?"

He retrieved the trousers he'd hung over the footpost and dug for the pocketwatch she knew he was never without, flicking it open. "Almost three. Far too early to get up." He tossed the watch aside and regarded her with shadowed eyes. "I could use more sleep, and I bet you could, too."

"I don't know if I could fall asleep."

"Sure, you can." He moved nearer to the bed and gently touched her shoulder. "Stretch out, right there." When she hesitantly obeyed, he tucked the blanket around her, then came to rest beside her, closer than he'd been earlier in the night when they'd first gone to bed.

She wanted his arms around her. "Joshua, I—"

"Whatever it is can wait for morning." He held out a palm to her.

She stared at his hand, strong, callused from hard work, darkly tanned from the sun, attached to a sinewy, muscled arm she already knew held plenty of power.

Lord, he was more than tempting against the rumpled sheets, bare chest gleaming in the lamp they'd left burning low on the bureau, all that golden-brown hair tangled on the pillow next to hers. She wanted to rub up against him so badly. Wanted to feel the heat of his body over every inch of her.

We're married. We're allowed to touch, to kiss. And more.

As to exactly what 'more' entailed, Vivian knew enough to understand her need to crawl into her husband's arms and make this a real marriage instead of what it had started out to be.

A way to save her reputation.

Duty. Responsibility. A chore.

How could she bear to be anyone's chore?

"Vivian?"

Meeting his questioning gaze, Vivian slowly took his outstretched hand. Her churning thoughts slowed when he squeezed gently, warmth in his gaze. It was obvious he cared for her, at least a little.

I can work with that.

Joshua leaned across the pillow and placed a light kiss high on her cheek. "Sweet dreams, angel."

~ ~ ~

"Auntie Vivian!"

Vivian looked up from the box of slate tablets the Lomans had donated and smiled happily at the sight of Addie Carter bouncing through the salon door, blond pigtails flying, her ruffled gingham smock already boasting a smear of dirt.

She set the tablets down and held out her arms, laughing when Addie leapt, arms and legs winding around her like a monkey. "Well, look at you. I'd say somebody's feeling much better."

Addie nodded eagerly. "I'm all better. 'Cept I think I gave the coop to Jenny."

"Croup," Vivian corrected, eyeing her niece's flushed

cheeks. "No more fever? No more coughing?"

"Nope. I'm ready to be in school and Mama says I'm not 'tagious."

"Contagious."

"Yep, I'm not that, neither." With a final squeeze that knocked the air from Vivian's lungs, Addie slithered to the floor and darted across the room, hollering, "Nate," at the top of her lungs. Nabbing the chair next to him at the table, the precocious imp wriggled in place, beaming when he obligingly slid his brand-new reader aside to make room for her. He tousled her hair teasingly, murmuring something that made her shriek with glee.

"I have missed that little sunbeam," Mama commented as she came up beside the desk the Stage House had loaned for daily class. She scooped up the chalk and tablets. "I'll just pass these out, shall I?"

"Thank you, Mama." Vivian collected the remainder of the new readers from their makeshift shelf against the wall and set them out. The children would have to share for a while, until an additional order came in from back East, but she knew none of her students minded doubling up.

She gazed out at the overly-warm yet cozy salon, thankful anew that Catherine had donated space for her use. She hadn't a clue when work would begin on the new schoolhouse, though the town had begun a fund drive and had managed to save about a third of the overall cost. In the meantime she had a comfortable place to teach, a solid start to new supplies thanks to Silas and Betsey, and the children enjoyed a hot meal each day, compliments of Mary Rush, the Stage House's wonderful cook.

With no assigned seating, the girls and boys mostly paired off haphazardly, though at playtime they'd congregate together outside and engage in kick the can or tag. At least one girl's dress would rend at the seam or hem, and someone would end up with scraped knees. Vivian would break up arguments, soothe hurt feelings, or tickle a sullen child into giggles. At the end of the day each student would skip out the door with a cheery farewell, the girls lining up to hug her and the boys snickering at the silliness of the girls.

I love every minute of it.

"All right, everyone." Vivian raised her voice to be heard over the chatter. "Time to practice our number tables." At the collective groans, she winked at Mama, leaning against the door leading to the kitchen. "If you all do well, Missus Carter just might have cookies to share." She smothered a chuckle when the groans changed to whoops and cheers, thinking what a fine thing it could be if adults were made happy with the simple offer of a cookie or two.

With the younger children busily working their fives and sixes, the older ones practicing multiplications, Vivian rose and stretched her back, wandering to the window overlooking the side lawn. The day had been overcast but it hadn't yet rained, and she hoped that state would hold at least through playtime. Otherwise she'd be dealing with a roomful of rambunctiousness.

Her attention was abruptly caught by the sight of a nattily-garbed fellow in a deep gray coat and striped trousers, boots polished to a blinding gleam, striding up the street, one meaty hand clutching a bouquet of flowers. Thinking it was Knight Gleason headed for the bank and planning a surprise for Hannah Penderson, Vivian spared a smile for the kind, if a bit oblivious lady.

Then she looked again, realizing the man's hair was silver-streaked, instead of Mister Gleason's Irish red. Squinting, Vivian all but pressed her nose to the glass.

My goodness.

Dub Blackwood, cleanly shaven and dressed like a dandy, strode toward the Stage House. As he drew closer, the look on his weathered face became very clear. A man determined, once and for all, to get his woman.

"Oh, Mama," Vivian muttered, breaking into a wide grin. "You're in trouble now."

~ ~ ~

When Joshua stepped inside the Stage House to collect Vivian and Nate, loud chatter and childish screeches greeted him. Removing his dusty hat, he knocked it against his leg and strode to the side salon where Vivian normally set up her class. He was early, but figured he'd grab a piece of pie in the kitchen while he waited.

He'd no sooner gained the salon doorway than Nate, followed by Addie Carter, tore around the corner and barreled into him, both talking at once.

"I'm getting a new grandpa, Uncle Sheriff—"

Nate interrupted with, "Missus Lucinda said yes."

Addie nodded until her pigtails danced. "We're having another wedding, and Mama says I can wear my hair up."

"Whoa, one at a time." Joshua slung an arm around each squirming child and held them in place as two happy faces stared up at him. "Tell me everything," he teased Addie, who puffed up with a huge breath as if ready to explode.

"Mister Dub asked Grammy, all proper-like, and he even got down on one knee and gave her a bunch of flowers. And he asked like this." Addie adopted a prayerful pose and deepened her voice. "'Lucinda, darlin', for the love of God marry me.' And he looked sort of scared and—"

Nate jumped in, "Then Missus Lucinda started crying, and she got down on *her* knees and hugged Mister Dub and said of course I will, you foolish man, and then Missus Vivian and Missus Catherine started crying, too." His cheeks flushed with excitement. "Missus Vivian says now I have to get new shoes, and prob'ly a shirt, so I can look presentable."

Addie wormed her way between Nate and Joshua. "Can

Nate wear a pink shirt to match my new dress?" At the boy's look of horror, she pouted. "I think pink is pretty."

It was all Joshua could do to keep a straight face. "Uh, I believe we can let Nate pick his own shirt, Miss Adeline." He guided the children into the room with a hand to each shoulder, heading toward the main salon where the noise was loudest. "Are y'all having a party back there?"

Nate nodded vigorously. "Missus Vivian stopped school when Mister Dub came in, looking for Missus Lucinda. He had to go up and down the stairs twice to find her. Missus Vivian said she wasn't going to miss this, and we all got to stand at the door and watch." His nose wrinkled. "It was fun, but they were kissing and stuff, too. It got pretty mushy."

Addie poked him with a bony elbow. "Wasn't mushy."

"Was so." Nate danced away, tauntingly, with Addie running after him. His laughter and her shrieks rang in the quiet schoolroom as they chased each other in circles.

"Did you hear?" Vivian came up beside him, her face glowing. "I'm getting a new papa."

Joshua curved his arm around her shoulders. "I heard. Did the man at least shave for the event?"

"Yes, but even better—"she tugged him toward the side door—"he got all fancied up. Wait 'til you see."

Joshua let her drag him along, then stood at the wide entrance to the main salon and blinked at the sight of Dub Blackwood, tough silver miner, duded up like a high-class gent, sitting next to Lucinda Carter with an enormous grin. He held her hand as if doting on a queen, placing a kiss on the inside palm while she blushed like a young girl. All around the elegant room, Vivian's students gobbled cookies and slurped glasses of what looked like lemonade, while Frank and Catherine chatted with Betsey, Mary, and a few of the Stage House servers.

"Dub didn't even ask Frank or Harrison for permission,"

Vivian confided, hugging Joshua's arm to her chest and making him painfully aware of the softly rounded curve of her breasts hidden beneath her pretty striped blouse. "Came in and stomped around until he found Mama. He dropped to his knees, right here in the salon. I've never seen a more desperate man."

Joshua understood completely. Regardless of the circumstances, he was desperate to do right by the lovely young woman who'd come into his life. Snagging her around the waist, he drew her close, rubbing his lips against the delicate lobe of her ear. "Looks like Little Creede has another new bride."

With Vivian's sweet fragrance making his head swim, he wondered how much longer he'd be able to resist taking her to his bed for more than just sleeping. Images of the rough couplings he'd enjoyed over the years made him grind his back teeth together.

No way in hell I'll ever touch Vivian that way.

Until he was sure he could treat her with the tenderness she deserved, he'd remain on his own damn side of the bed.

Chapter 13

Vivian's jaw dropped as she stepped into the main salon at the Stage House. "Goodness, I've never seen so much food."

Joshua hefted the cloth-covered basket he'd brought in from the wagon. "Tell me again what we're doing." He carried the basket to a table already groaning under the weight of cakes and assorted pastries, and set it on the floor. Whisking off the cloth, he lifted out pie after pie, edging them onto the only open spot available. "Six pies. Who's going to eat all of this?"

"The entire town, I suspect." Vivian deposited the smaller basket she'd carried, containing loaves of bread, and surveyed the overloaded tables. "It's a fund-raising potluck. If folks want to eat, they donate money. We used to have these potlucks all the time back in Stanley. Once, we raised enough money to rebuild a church that'd collapsed during a nasty winter storm. It was smart of Mama to remember."

As she unpacked the loaves she'd baked, Joshua ambled around the room, peering at the covered dishes, linen-wrapped platters, and boxes. "There must be twenty baked chickens over here." He chuckled. "About as many hams, too."

"Well, Mary and Betsey have been busy. I heard Betsey nagged Ike Barnes until he donated one of his steers for meat. Nellie sent word that the mine families will come to town in shifts so they can all have a meal. Rocky Gulch, too. I promise you, nobody will go hungry today."

They shared a smile over the expanse of the salon.

"Angel, you'll have that money raised for your new school in no time."

"Oh, I hope so."

A few minutes later Mama swept in, wearing her favorite red watered silk, Dub beaming as he held her hand. "You're both finally here. Joshua, do you mind helping with the champagne? In the side salon. Bring in, oh, let's see." She pondered a moment. "Just bring it all in."

"Thirty bottles? You think it's enough?" Dub asked.

Vivian gasped, "Champagne, Mama? For a simple potluck?"

"Oh, darling," her mother purred, "not just a potluck." She laid her left hand, with its sparkling sapphire betrothal ring, against Dub's grinning face. "It's our engagement party, too."

~ ~ ~

An hour later the potluck was in full swing, with most of the town either clustered around the food tables, spilling out into the lobby, the staircase and half-landing, or standing and sitting, even on the floor. Plates were heaped with chicken and ham, beans, sugared carrots and squash, biscuits dripping in redeye gravy, all balanced in laps or crowded on any free surface. The yeasty smell of baked bread filled the air.

Joshua stood with Vivian, both of them finished with their plates and having willingly given up their seats so others could sit and eat at leisure. Behind him, Frank's low rumble and Catherine's lilting responses blended with Addie's constant chatter as she sat on the floor and helped Jenny strip the meat from a chicken leg.

For the first time in days, Joshua allowed himself to relax. Life out at the ranch had evened to a stable pace, with no further disturbances from Nate's mother. Other than tossing rowdy drunks in jail to sober up or arresting sore-loser gamblers over at the Galleria, Joshua and his deputies were able to cover patrolling the town as well as rotate out at both mines.

Maybe such calm wouldn't last that long, but in the meantime, Joshua intended to enjoy this time with his wife and his foster son.

He'd just leaned in close to Vivian's ear to relay an amusing tidbit he'd overheard, when Knight Gleason swept through the wide doorway of the main salon. On his arm, a radiant Hannah, dressed in soft blue, smiled and waved to folks who called out friendly greetings. Joshua regarded the once-dowdy bank teller with fondness. Hannah had really blossomed since the burly Georgian had set his cap for her.

Behind them, a beautifully turned-out young lady entered alongside an older gent with silver-steaked hair. Joshua noted the brilliant red of her upswept locks and wagered this must be Gleason's niece. Miranda? Melinda?

No, Magnolia. A nice Southern name for certain. She clung to the arm of the man who must be her father. Shorter, rather stoop-shouldered, the man nonetheless escorted his daughter with solicitous care, his face turned to hers as she looked around with wide eyes.

As Knight stopped to shake hands with Silas, his family members strolled closer, the niece offering the kind of sweet, yet vague smile women often adopt when in a room filled with strangers. Her father paused to allow a giggling toddler to dash by, and when he looked up again, his bespectacled gaze fell on Joshua. For a long moment he stared, then his bushy brows drew together in a thunderous frown and he started forward, leaving his daughter's side.

Joshua almost turned to peer behind him to see who might have put such anger on the man's face, when he realized the fury was all for him. Sensing danger, he dropped his arm from around Vivian's waist, steeling himself for an upcoming battle he didn't understand.

"*You.*" The man actually bumped boots with him. "What're you doin' around these fine folks?" His dismissive glare raked Joshua, pausing at chest-level. "You're the *sheriff*?" His face pinched, as if he'd just eaten something bitter.

Joshua fruitlessly wracked his brain for a memory that would explain this man's contempt. "Do I know you?"

"I'd say you do." The man's lips twisted into a sneer. "How the hell did a little perverted pissant like you end up policing a town?"

The verbal attack rendered him speechless. It'd been a long time since Joshua had been taken so unawares.

Frank appeared behind Vivian. "What in hell is going on here?" He sized up Knight's red-faced relative. "Who are you?"

Before the man could speak, Knight hurried over. "Bubba, what're yew hollerin' about?" He settled a heavy palm on the man's shoulder. "Gents, this is mah sister's widower, Percy Sanders. He's mah sweet Magnolia's daddy." He nodded toward his niece, now seated at a table chatting with Hannah.

He spun 'Bubba' around none-too-gently. "Yew wanna explain yerself, hollerin' at mah friends?"

"I'd like to hear this, too." Harrison had stepped to Joshua's side. "But I don't think the entire town needs to listen in. Shall we take this to a more private room?"

~ ~ ~

In the visiting salon, Vivian sank onto a velvet-tufted settee. Catherine had followed her in, sitting close to her and catching hold of her hand.

"Cold," Catherine murmured, stroking a thumb over Vivian's knuckles. "Whatever it is, we'll get to the bottom of it." She regarded the clot of men, standing in a circle several feet away. "Any idea what's going on?"

"Not a clue." Vivian gently pulled her hand from Catherine's warm clasp. "But if it involves Joshua, then I'm going to find out." Rising, she crossed to her husband's side and took his arm.

He turned to her, looking a bit pale. "Angel, you should go back to the party—"

"Are you his wife?" Sanders barked out.

Joshua's head snapped back around, and a growl rumbled from his throat. "Watch your tone, mister."

"It's all right, Joshua." Vivian spoke soothingly, trying to ease the tension in the room. She eyed the red-faced Sanders. "I'm Vivian Lang, yes."

"I'm sorry, young lady. I meant no offense." Sanders threw Joshua a look of disgust. "But you have my sympathies, because your husband isn't fit for regular society—"

"You'd better have something to back that up," Frank growled. "I've known Joshua for over six years. He's been the town sheriff most of that time and does a damned fine job of it. He's also family." He jerked his chin toward a glowering Harrison. "Vivian's our sister."

Sanders blanched at that but didn't back down. "I came across this miscreant years ago, in Texas. He was a bordello rat. Young and dumb to be sure, but that doesn't excuse the way he pandered to the shady ladies. Disgraceful." At Vivian's swift intake of breath, Sanders mustered an apologetic demeanor. "I am sorry to upset you, Missus Lang, but you should know the kind of man you've married."

"You're mistaken," she began heatedly.

"Bullshit," Harrison growled.

Knight muttered a rumbling, "Yew better shut yer mouth, Bubba—"

"*No.*" Joshua's low rebuttal cut through. The muscles of his arm stiffened, until they felt like stone beneath Vivian's fingers. She turned to him and all the air left her lungs at the bleak look in his eyes.

Catherine had appeared at Vivian's elbow, her emerald gaze steady as she took in the tense group. "Let me just say, gentlemen, the past belongs in the past, and all of us have a skeleton or two."

Joshua exhaled roughly. "You're right." Easing from Vivian's death grip, he curved his arm around her waist and brought her close. "I was born in Texas. Grew up in a Galveston whorehouse." When she gasped, he hugged her tighter to his side. "It wasn't an easy life. My ma was a drunk and a whore. I never knew my pa. And I was just a young'un, four, close to five, when my ma was murdered by one of her customers."

"Oh, Joshua." Vivian couldn't begin to fathom such a life for a young child.

Harrison started to speak but subsided when Joshua held up a hand.

He faced Sanders squarely. "I won't ask you how you came to be in that place when I was a boy. That's your business. Once my ma died, the other whores took care of me. Some were kind. Others, not so much. When I got big enough, they began to treat me like a plaything, a toy for them to pass around. At first, I didn't understand. Didn't take me long to figure out it wasn't right. I knew I had to get away, so I stole some coins from the owner's strongbox, and ran."

The more Joshua talked, the whiter Sander's face grew. "Son, I'm sorry. I had no way of knowing . . ."

Joshua gave a curt nod. "I understand. But as you can see, I've made a better life for myself."

Chapter 14

Joshua secured the reins and threw the wheel brake before jumping down from the bench seat. Vivian couldn't take her eyes from his muscular frame as he strode around the front of the wagon, checking Tinker's harness and adjusting the strap over the stallion's broad back.

Coming around to her side, he held up his arms. "Down we go, angel."

Gripping her waist, Joshua easily swung her from the seat, quickly releasing her to turn away to check the horses.

Vivian almost growled in frustration. Just when their marriage had begun to make some headway, that awful man had confronted her husband at the potluck dinner.

Joshua had been avoiding her ever since.

Vivian would never hold his past against him. As Catherine said, what was in the past, stayed there. What mattered was how one conducted their lives today, and Joshua Lang was, in all things, a good man.

She sighed. Married three weeks, come Friday . . . *And my own mama is a newer bride but more a wife than I am.*

Vivian choked back fresh frustration.

Six days ago, Mama and Dub exchanged vows in a quiet church ceremony. Wearing a deep blue gown with delicate beading that perfectly matched her betrothal ring, she simply glowed as she faced her bridegroom in the soft light from a dozen candles.

Because the fund-raising potluck had become an engagement celebration, the new Mister and Missus Blackwood had foregone a reception and instead had left right after the wedding, traveling by stage to catch an eastbound train for Stanley, the little home town in Illinois they'd left behind when they'd moved to Colorado. Mama didn't have a lot of family left on her side, but Aunt Prudence and Uncle Edgar still lived right down the road from what used to be the Carter homestead, and Mama wanted to introduce her new husband to those relatives remaining in the area.

Vivian was happy to help out at the Stage House each day, between school hours and over the weekend when the dining salon was especially busy. Catherine had offered the use of a suite on the second floor, right down the hall from the rooms she shared with Frank and little Charity. The two attached bedrooms had already come in handy once, when duty had Joshua delayed at the jail and they'd ended up spending the night in town. Vivian had curled up on the chaise with her embroidery while Nate worked on his schoolbooks. She recalled how comfortable she'd felt, waiting for her husband in the warm, cozy sitting room.

In the days following Joshua's revelation of his childhood, Vivian noticed a distinct softening in her brothers' attitudes toward him. Whatever gaps remained in Joshua's past, Frank and Harrison were able to put their initial distrust aside.

Though Percy Sanders hadn't stopped by the Stage House, Vivian had seen his daughter once or twice, strolling through town with Hannah. At least Knight Gleason's kin hadn't spoken another harsh word against Joshua.

As for Joshua himself, he'd not revealed anything else. Vivian suspected more, but she wasn't about to push.

Her attention refocused on Nate as he hopped down from the back of the wagon, followed by the faithful Tansy, her tail wagging madly. His smile was as bright as the sun as he asked, "Can I run over to the mercantile for one of Missus Loman's cookies? Tansy can come with me."

Vivian bit her bottom lip worriedly. She'd been unwilling to let him out of her sight ever since his mother had tried to snatch him off the street. The woman hadn't been seen in many days, and everyone hoped she'd gone back to wherever she'd come from. "I don't know . . ."

Joshua ruffled the top of the boy's head. "That's fine, partner. Keep alert for trouble, though. And I'll come get you, so stay there until you see me, all right?"

Nate nodded solemnly, for an instant looking far too adult for his tender age, then his little boy grin was back. "I promise."

He took off running, with Tansy barking and nipping at his heels. His childish laughter cut through the air and warmed her heart, even as her gaze anxiously followed him.

"He'll be fine," Joshua promised, reaching out to cup her cheek. For the first time in weeks, his gaze held the tenderness she'd been missing. "I have eyes on this town, remember? The Blackwood brothers are deputized now."

Vivian brought her hand up to cover his, not wanting to lose this connection with him, everything inside her willing him to kiss her.

As if reading her mind, his gaze grew warm. He leaned in and tenderly pressed his mouth against hers in a soft kiss.

Vivian closed her eyes, reveling at the feel of his lips on hers, and needing more. More of his kisses. More of his touches. Just . . . more.

"I'll be back to pick you up around suppertime," he murmured against her mouth.

She soaked up the magical moment, even as his lips lifted from hers. That now-familiar yearning, welling up inside her, left her aching in the most peculiar ways. Oh, how she wished she knew how to seduce her husband.

"Angel, are you listening?" Amusement threaded Joshua's voice.

Her eyes flew open to find him studying her with clear affection. "We'll eat at the Stage House tonight, like a real family. You, me, and Nate." He brushed a tiny kiss over the end of her nose before drawing away. "Sound good?"

That quickly, happiness filled her up. Joshua might not be claiming her as his wife yet, but he had claimed her and Nate as his family. The rest would come, in time.

"Yes, very good. Thank you, Joshua."

"You go on in, now."

Vivian nodded, shooting a glance toward the mercantile to see if Nate made it inside safely. This far away, she couldn't see through the windows.

"He's fine," Joshua assured her. "I don't want you worrying."

They locked eyes, and her breath caught at the way his gaze darkened. She thought he might kiss her again, but instead he stepped back. "I'll see you at supper."

She nodded, but didn't move, unable to look away from him.

His lips curved enticingly in response. Hands clasping her shoulders, he spun her toward the Stage House. "Go on now. I won't forget to collect Nate from Betsey's and walk him over."

"All right." Vivian closed the distance to the Stage House, then glanced back to see Joshua standing where she'd left him, watching her. She gave him a little wave.

Catherine met her near the entrance. "Hello, sister dear." She peered over Vivian's shoulder. "Where's Nate?"

"He stopped by Betsey's for a treat. Joshua will bring him over soon."

"I left a few books upstairs for him I thought he'd enjoy."

"I'm sure he will. Thank you. The boy does love to read."

"Who knows?" Catherine said with a shrug. "Maybe he'll be an author someday."

Vivian beamed, feeling every bit like a proud mama. "I wouldn't put it past him."

Trudy hurried over just then, looking harried. "I'm sorry, Missus Catherine, but one of the guests is demanding to see the owner." She nervously ran her hands down the skirt of her uniform. "Told everyone he's in town for a gambling tourney and heard we're the best restaurant around. Now he's refusing to pay because he says the breakfast eggs were overdone."

"Were they?" Catherine asked.

Trudy shook her head. "No, ma'am. They were perfect as usual."

"All right. I'll be in directly." Catherine sighed as Trudy returned to the main salon. "Ever since that gambling hall opened, I've had nothing but trouble. I swear, if one more gambler stumbles in after a night of drinking and complains about the food, I'm going to dump it over his head. As if they can even taste what they eat when their tongues are numbed by liquor."

Vivian chuckled, knowing Catherine might actually follow through on the threat. "Maybe you need to hire someone to watch the door. Make sure they don't get inside when they're drunk."

"Hmm, that's an idea." Catherine's features relaxed. "When Dub and Lucinda get back, I'll ask if he'd like the job." She snagged Vivian's hand and drew her in for a quick hug. "I'll see you at lunch, but for now I suppose I had best deal with this disgruntled fool." Pivoting with a swirl of her skirts, she moved toward the salon.

Vivian climbed the stairs to her room. With an hour before school began, she had a bit of time to tidy up. Moving to the chifforobe where clean sheets were usually kept, she opened the bottom, largest drawer, but found it empty. Patsy must have forgotten to restock the linens, probably not used to the suite being occupied.

Vivian checked the middle drawer, also empty. When she opened the top one, expecting to find nothing there as well, she spied a dark object tucked at the back. Curious, she retrieved it, pulling out a leather-bound book.

Turning it over, she inhaled sharply at the image of a naked man and woman on the front cover, entwined in a lovers' pose. Her first instinct was to shove the book back where she'd gotten it, until her curiosity took over. Flipping through the pages, her heart raced at the shocking drawings, their detail exquisitely rendered. The accompanying text was in a language she couldn't identify, but perhaps words were not needed. Not when the drawings enlightened so . . . explicitly.

Good Lord.

With rapt attention, her cheeks heating furiously, she studied the surprisingly beautiful images, wondering if a body could even bend that way.

A rapid knock at the door made her jump guiltily. Shoving the book back in place, she rushed over to fling the door open, surprised to find Maude Adams standing there. The solemn look on the woman's normally smiling face concerned her. "Maude, what is it?"

"It's Buck." Her voice quavered alarmingly, and for a moment she looked like she'd collapse, then her hunched shoulders straightened, her chin lifting with dignity and determination. "He'd like to see you."

Oh, no. The man's health had been deteriorating rapidly, though he kept up a brave face whenever Vivian stopped by for a chat. Which had increased to at least once a day over most of September, because she'd been so worried about him.

Vivian nodded, placing her arms around Maude's fragile frame in a comforting hug. "Of course."

She held Maude's arm as they descended the wide staircase, and for once the elderly woman let someone else help her.

At the bottom Catherine stood, looking worried. "I'll be back in an hour," Vivian said, then paused. "Nate's still over at the mercantile."

"He's here, don't worry. I saw Joshua walk him over. They dropped off a tray of pies for Mary," Catherine assured her. "I'll keep an eye on your boy until you return."

Less than ten minutes later Vivian entered the bedroom Maude and Buck had shared from the first day they'd opened the boardinghouse. Her heart clutched in dread at his appearance, worse than her last visit with him only yesterday afternoon.

His sunken eyes lit when he saw her.

Hurrying over, she took a seat in the rocking chair next to his bed and clasped his hand between her palms, swallowing back her panic at his weakened state. "Mr. Adams—Buck," she stammered, "I'm here, dear friend."

~ ~ ~

The creak of the jailhouse door roused Joshua from the paperwork he'd been tussling with. He looked up as Ben stepped into the stuffy room. The stoic expression on his deputy's face had Joshua jumping to his feet, his first thoughts centered on Vivian and Nate, scared one of them had been hurt. "What?"

"It's Buck Adams. He's passed, and your wife is mighty upset." His face was etched with grief.

Ah, shit. His own worries over the way his past followed him to Little Creede fell away under the weight of such a tragedy.

Vivian and Buck had grown close over the last year, even more so lately. His bride had a heart as big as Colorado, and she'd taken the older gentleman under her tender wing, instinctively knowing his time on earth was short. Still, she'd be devastated over his death. No one was ever truly prepared.

"Thanks, Ben." Joshua snatched up his Stetson. "Do you know if she's still with Maude?"

"No, Catherine brought her back to the Stage House. A bunch of the neighbor ladies are taking care of Maude right now. Dub went to notify Harrison, and Betsey's watching the children until their folks can get them from class."

Joshua nodded his thanks as he exited the jail. Already, a group of women were clustered on the porch of the boardinghouse, some going inside to comfort the widow. Buck and Maude's marriage was one of the longest he'd ever known, fifty years, and his heart clenched with sympathy over the horrendous loss.

He strode through the double doors of the Stage House, nodding to Trudy as she wiped away tears and pointed up the stairs. He took them two at a time and hurried down the hall to the guest suite, entering quietly. Vivian sat on the bed, crying her heart out in Catherine's arms.

Catherine met his gaze over Vivian's shoulder, her eyes glassy with emotion. Joshua murmured his thanks, then slid into place, exchanging Catherine's arms for his own. Vivian barely reacted as he pulled her close, whispering words of comfort as the sound of the door shutting gave them privacy.

"He's gone, Joshua," she sobbed against his chest. "He died while I was holding his hand." Her entire body shook with her grief, and he'd never felt more helpless in his life as he did his best to console his wife.

Lifting her onto his lap, he cradled her like a child and let her grieve.

~ ~ ~

Flo flinched when Slim caressed her bruised cheek. "If you'd done what you were told," he said gently, "I wouldn't have had to hurt you." Affection and cunning shone in his eyes as he stared down at her.

the kiss gentle, unwilling to take advantage of his wife in her distress.

As her husband, it was up to him to make her world better. If she were more experienced, he'd have her on her back, making love to her until she was too lost in passion to mourn and too caught up in his kisses to cry, unless it was to cry out in pleasure. He'd touch her in ways he'd been yearning to since the day they'd wed.

Today's not that day, Lang, he told himself, even as her lips parted and his tongue slid inside, greedy for the sweetness of her mouth. Passion grew between them like a prairie fire, bursting into something far more than he'd expected but was powerless to stop.

Minutes passed as Joshua's desire grew hotter and hotter, until he realized he'd shifted Vivian so that she straddled him, her womanly center pressed firmly against his cock, the only barriers between them the clothing they wore. Need slammed into him, and he instinctively thrust his hips forward and ground into the warmth between her thighs.

The sound of her answering whimper was enough to make him forget everything except the wonder of having Vivian in his arms. God, how he wanted her.

She's grieving, jackass. He had to stop. Breaking the kiss, Joshua feathered his lips across her cheek.

"Easy now, angel," he murmured, "we have all the time in the world." He stared into her passion-filled eyes, making the next words out of his mouth even harder since he'd never wanted her more than he did right now. "There's no need to rush."

"I don't want to wait." Her face flushed with desire, she pleaded, "You're my husband. I want our marriage to start. I don't wish to wait another minute when life is far too short. We've waited long enough."

She began working on the thin ribbons lacing the bodice of her nightgown. Mouth agape, Joshua froze as Vivian peeled away the soft fabric, until her breasts were fully exposed to him. His gaze fell to the perfect roundness of those firm globes, and as if by their own volition, his hands cupped them, rubbing his thumbs over the taut peaks.

Her needy, "Joshua," almost undid him.

He opened his mouth to again try and talk some sense into her, but she leaned in and kissed him, her tongue darting inside to tangle with his. What shocked him the most though, was when her hand slid down to grasp his hard length.

The promise he'd made to himself to give her time to decide if she wanted to stay in this marriage, given what she'd learned about him at the potluck, withered and died. Sweetheart that she was, Vivian didn't seem to hold his past against him. And he could no longer resist taking what her gaze so freely offered whenever she looked at him.

Once, he might have been able to do the right thing, walk away, even if it meant she married another, more suitable man. That time had now passed.

I'll never let her go, he silently acknowledged, as all his coherent thought fled south and pooled in his aching cock.

His little angel had turned into a demanding siren. With a groan Joshua barely recognized as coming from him, he shifted Vivian onto her back. For a moment, he could only stare down at the loveliness bared to his gaze.

His thumb traced her soft cheek, stained with residual tears. Her bottom lip quivered, though her eyes were clear and steady. The storm of emotion only made her more desirable to him.

So tenderhearted. So utterly feminine and sweet.

And all mine. Still, Joshua resisted the urge to crow aloud at his good fortune.

"Vivian," he began, only to stutter to a stop when she pressed a hand over his mouth.

"You went out in the rain and picked flowers for me." She moved her hand aside and replaced it with her mouth.

She didn't understand. If Mama were here, she could help, at least provide some answers. But Mama and Dub were still in Illinois. Even if they'd already left, it would take days of traveling by train and stagecoach until their return.

Now it was Friday. She and Joshua planned to stay over so he could catch up at the jail. Vivian would assist Catherine with the ledgers, one of Mama's duties as manager of the dining salon. Saturday evening, Joshua would escort her and Nate back to the ranch to deal with the horses and livestock. There would be little or no time to talk to him, find out why he'd changed toward her, just as she'd thought their marriage had finally become something real and true.

Sighing heavily, she stood just as Catherine breezed into the kitchen, pausing to stare at her. "What's wrong? I've seen happier corpses."

Despite her depression, Vivian managed a smile. Sometimes Catherine came up with the most colorful yet driest images. "Not quite a corpse." She paused thoughtfully. "If I asked you something, would you keep it to yourself?" Heat rose to her face as she amended, "I mean, keep it from—"

"Frank," Catherine finished with obvious amusement. "That's a nice shade of red you've got brewing on those cheeks of yours." Cool and collected as usual, she took a seat at a small side table. "Come sit and tell me what you don't want your brother to know."

Vivian plopped down. "Um." Words failing her, she twisted the sleeve of her shirtwaist into a knot.

Catherine laid a hand over hers, stilling its restlessness. "Stop that and talk to me."

"I just—" Frustrated, Vivian blurted, "Why are husbands so difficult?"

"Why, what did Joshua do?"

"Nothing, and therein lies the problem." Vivian sighed.

"Just when we begin to make some progress in our marriage, he backs away."

"Was it after the ugly incident at the potluck?"

"No, we worked that out."

"Glad to hear it. He worked it out with your brothers, too."

"He did?"

Catherine nodded. "Frank told me about it. They assured your husband that not a single person holds what happened to him as a child against him." She clasped Vivian's fingers in a comforting squeeze. "Keep in mind, you're married to the man who protects the entire town, and I'm sure that protection triples when it comes to you. And you're young."

Vivian twisted away, scowling. "I bet Frank doesn't treat you like a child."

Catherine blew out a sigh, leaning back in her chair. "Viv, I wasn't as young as you when I *was* as young as you. I grew up early and fast. You've been sheltered most of your life. A certificate of teaching doesn't change the fact that your family can't see past the girl to accept the woman. A similar attitude rubbed off on your husband. It might not be fair, but there you go."

"He didn't treat me like a little girl the other night," Vivian snapped, fed up.

"Ah." Catherine nodded. "Now we're getting somewhere."

"I need some advice, Catherine. I'd ask Mama if she were here." Vivian held her gaze. "But you can't tell Frank."

"I'd never say a thing to your brother. Either of them, and you know what? Neither would Retta. How about this?" Catherine tugged her to her feet and enveloped her in a warm hug. "It's been a while since we've had a good old-fashioned gab session. Tomorrow night, we'll clear out the menfolk and have ourselves a sleepover, what do you say? We'll take over your place and toss blankets on the floor in front of the fire. Eat cake in our nightgowns. Maybe drink some of that elderberry wine Nell Washburn made last year. It ought to be pretty well corked by now."

"I'd like that. You think we can talk the men into leaving us in peace for one night?"

"Probably not." Catherine chuckled. "But we'll do it anyway. They can drink and gamble to their hearts' content. Aunt Millie might love a chance to babysit, and I'd bet Nate would be glad to help out, too." Her smile grew into a mischievous grin. "Can you imagine, taking turns diapering those wild twins? That'd keep those overbearing husbands of ours busy."

"What a thing to wish on unsuspecting men." But Vivian felt a smile of her own breaking over her melancholy.

"You bet it is." Catherine gave her cheek a gentle pinch. "Come on, let's head upstairs. It's getting late and I need to nurse Charity." She moved toward the door leading to the lobby.

"Soon as I grab a bite for Nate. I promised him a treat for doing so well with his reader." Vivian stepped to the bin where Mary kept the leftover treats, lifting the lid and digging out a handful of sugar cookies.

As she turned to follow Catherine out, she caught a flicker at the half-open window. Vivian frowned at the darkness beyond, realizing she'd been in the kitchen much longer than she'd thought.

Probably someone having a final smoke before retiring. Dorrie, one of the daily servers, had taken up cheroots, much to Catherine's disapproval, but at least she did it outside.

Setting the plate on the table, Vivian shut the window before snuffing the wicks on the wall sconces. With no idea if Joshua was still at the jail or actually upstairs with Nate, she collected the sugary treat and hurried out.

~ ~ ~

"I don't like this," Frank grumbled, pacing Harrison's kitchen.

"Neither do I," Harrison replied, "but I promised Retta a long time ago if she ever wanted time for herself, I'd give it to her. Besides, we haven't had a game in months." Shuffling the cards, he nodded toward Joshua, kicked back in his chair. "You gonna loosen your bullets, Sheriff?"

"Hell, no." Joshua leaned forward. "I'm not real comfy myself, leaving the women alone."

Robert Blackwood rose, tossing down his cards. "Your women'll be fine. They're only a few hundred yards past the back fence, and Richard promised to keep an eye on 'em for you." He slapped on his Stetson and fastened the leg straps on his double holster. "I'm off to town to spell Ben."

Joshua rubbed the tight ball of tension in his neck. "If you'd check on the women before you head for town, I'd appreciate it." Though he was in no mood to play poker, he'd also made a promise to his wife. An evening with her new 'sisters' was something she needed, no matter how uneasy it made him. "And tell your brother thanks for doing guard duty tonight."

Robert gave an acknowledging nod. "You gents have a good game. Win big." Whistling tunelessly, he shut the door, boots clomping on the porch.

"All right, ladies, y'all finished making nice?" Harrison dealt speedily as Frank dragged a chair up to the table. "Let's get back to it. Five-card straight. Dollar to open. And no whooping, or else you'll wake the young'uns and Aunt Millie'll have my head."

Frank dropped some coins to start the opening pot. He glanced Harrison's way. "Wanna take bets on how long it'll be before Retta pops out another babe?"

In unison, they lifted their drinks, draining the whiskey before placing the shot glasses back on the table with a thud.

Harrison poured refills all around, then recorked the bottle of Old James. His face split wide with a grin. "For all I know she might already be with child. I'm a fortunate man."

Joshua dug into his pocket for a coin and flipped it on the table. "If y'all end up with more bottoms to diaper, might be enough to pull those burrs out of your asses over me marrying Vivian."

Both men grumbled, tossing more silver on the pile and threatening to cut off certain strategic parts of his body if he hurt their little sister.

Scooping up his cards, Joshua vaguely noted the beginnings of a royal flush. But superimposed over his one-eyed jack was Vivian's pretty face and the faint, sad smile she'd given him after he'd escorted her to the ranch and brushed a kiss on her upturned mouth.

Regret sat in his gut like a lead ball. Trying to be the gentleman toward his wife was damned hard, when all he wanted to do was toss her back in their bed for some more of what he'd gotten the other night.

Joshua frowned and tossed a couple more coins into the pot. He longed to claim her again but he wasn't an animal, despite his unorthodox introduction to bedroom sport, and his regrettable couplings over the years.

And he didn't want Vivian thinking his possession of her body was all he desired, because he wanted so much more from her, from this marriage. Complicating how he'd already mucked things up was his inability to fix it.

He bit back a sigh. *Hell, it's gonna be a long night.*

~ ~ ~

Retta took one whiff of the jug in her hands and gagged. "Oh, awful. Smells like vinegar. We can't drink this." She shoved the cork back in place and set it aside. "Coffee it is."

"I'll make it." Vivian jumped up and hurried into the kitchen, happy to be doing something with her hands.

Reaching above the dish rack for the tin of grounds and the strainer, she concentrated on the mindless task while in the front room, Catherine nursed a sleepy-eyed Charity and chatted softly with Retta.

Tying one of Mama's old aprons over her dressing gown to keep it clean, Vivian bent half an ear to the bits of conversation floating in, Retta's concern for Maude Adams' ability to keep the boardinghouse going the uppermost topic. With no children to help out, Maude would need the town's support more than ever. Vivian spared a fond thought for the couple whose long marriage had been an inspiration for many. Both Maude and Buck shared—at times—a rather bawdy sense of humor, and more than once Vivian had been witness to bickering that ended in a kiss from Maude on Buck's wrinkled cheek. Once, he'd swatted her on her backside as she'd crossed the room, stepping within reach of his rocking chair. Instead of taking exception, she'd cackled and called him an old coot.

I want that kind of marriage. Fun and maybe sometimes a bit naughty.

Vivian filled the coffee pot with water and set it on the cookstove, stirring up the embers from supper and adding more kindling. She still hadn't confided anything to Catherine or Retta, and as the evening progressed, she wondered if she could.

The leather-bound book she'd brought home from the Stage House, now safely tucked away at the bottom of her lingerie drawer, came to mind. As she carefully placed the heavy copper grinder onto the table, her cheeks heated, remembering the drawings on the pages inside.

Lord save her . . . if she couldn't even speak of the vaguest topics on marriage, how in the world could she reveal to them what was in that book?

Giving up on the coffee, Vivian whisked off the apron and returned to the front room with the remainder of the blueberry crisp Retta had baked earlier. She sank down next to Catherine, smiling when Charity gurgled, her eyes still that soft, newborn blue. Though Vivian wagered they'd go green soon enough.

"Want to lay her down?" Catherine expertly shifted the warm, sweet-smelling bundle to Vivian's eager arms. "On second thought," she mused, grinning, "why don't I finish the coffee and you can rock her for a bit?"

"Gladly." Vivian settled on the sofa and hummed softly as her niece yawned, thick lashes the color of straw sweeping over her cheeks, until she was fast asleep with a tiny snore and a dribble of milk at the corner of her mouth.

Retta came over and sat next to Vivian, brushing a tender kiss to Charity's strawberry-blond head. "She already looks so much like Catherine. Poor Frank won't let her out of the house until she's forty."

"I don't doubt it." Vivian pressed her cheek to the downy curls as longing for a child of her own overwhelmed her.

It's what I want, a family with Joshua.

"Won't happen unless the man is willing to touch me more than once," she mumbled.

"What?" Retta nudged her.

Vivian made a show of smoothing Charity's frilly sleeping sacque. "Nothing, I—"

A sudden, loud pop made them both jump. Retta pushed Vivian to the floor. "Stay down!"

"Was that a gunshot?" Vivian cradled Charity against her chest, wedging herself between the sofa and its matching footrest. From the corner of her eye she spotted Catherine crawling toward her.

"Are the doors locked?" Catherine asked urgently.

Vivian nodded. "And the windows are shut."

The sound of breaking glass killed that reassurance, and Vivian smothered a cry. "What on earth is going on?"

"No idea." Wriggling on her stomach, Catherine made her way toward the glass-plated rifle cabinet in the corner. "Vivian, which one is loaded?"

"All of them."

When more bullets tore into the room, Vivian clapped a hand over her heart.

Catherine wrenched the door open, catching a rifle by its stock. "Here." She motioned to Retta. "Grab one." She turned to Vivian. "Protect my child, Viv."

"With my life." Vivian snatched one of Aunt Millie's knitted throws off a nearby chair and covered herself and the babe with it. Amazingly, Charity slept on as if nothing was happening.

She wanted to join the fight against whoever was outside, threatening her family. But Retta and Catherine were deadly shots, plus Catherine could throw a knife with perfect aim. Surely the men would hear the gunfire and come running. They weren't that far away.

Retta crouched at a back window, poking the repeater through a broken pane and shooting.

More bullets whizzed through the kitchen window, lodging in the narrow wall separating both rooms. Biting back the urge to scream, Vivian tucked herself against the sofa so that Charity was completely shielded. A soft snuffle indicated the child still slept.

Carefully, Vivian raised her head, spotting Catherine on the other side of the room closest to the front door, firing through another broken pane.

"I can't see anything," Catherine snarled, in that moment sounding every bit as deadly as Frank, "but when I find out who's doing this, they're dead, I guarantee."

Vivian bent over Charity and prayed hard.

A volley of bullets from Catherine's rifle brought on a sharp cry from somewhere outside the front. "Got you, you bastard," she crowed, then ducked as a burst of gunfire ripped into the wall close to where Vivian lay with Charity. "Vivian, watch out!"

"We're safe," she answered shakily. "Retta," she called out, "Where are you?"

No answer. "Retta, oh, my Lord."

"I'm all right. Stay down. I hear our men coming."

Charity stirred and whimpered. "Shh, darling," Vivian soothed, rocking the fretful infant, now half-awake and squirming.

A large hand dropped on her shoulder and she shrieked, rolling away with Charity as the woolen throw tangled around her. "No!"

"It's me, angel."

Oh, thank goodness.

Frantically, she unwound herself and her niece from the suffocating throw and crawled into Joshua's arms, lightheaded with relief as they snapped around her and Charity, holding them tight. The babe emitted a yawn and a snore.

Vivian gave a strained laugh. "In all this, she merely slept."

"You took good care of her," Joshua murmured, burying his face in her hair. "Are you sure you're all right?"

"I've never been more scared, Joshua. Who was it?"

"Don't know. Frank and Harrison are out looking around." He broke off when Catherine rushed over, still crouched low. "They're fine, Catherine."

"Oh, Vivian, thank you." Catherine reached for her child, and Vivian handed her over. Her sister-by-marriage tried to speak further, gulped, and burst into tears.

Vivian gaped. She'd never seen Catherine cry, not even when she'd been shot and almost died, a scant year ago. But because these were mother-tears, Vivian understood.

Joshua helped her to her feet as the front door burst open and Frank tore inside. "Where are they? Cat, darlin', you gave me a turn." He bent and gathered both wife and child up into his arms. "You're not hurt? Christ almighty, when I find the bastard who did this—"

"Shh." Catherine placed a hand over his mouth. "Don't cuss in front of your daughter." She eased out of Frank's arms and unwrapped Charity, blinking at the snoring babe. "Probably never woke up once."

"Everyone all right?" Retta poked her head into the archway leading to the kitchen. "Harrison's outside looking for Richard." Her brow furrowed worriedly. "What if one of our bullets hit him?" She ventured closer, and when Frank held out his free arm, she burrowed in.

"Found him," Harrison called from the front porch, "behind the shade tree. Looks like he caught a bullet in the leg."

Already shaky on her feet, Catherine swayed alarmingly. "Oh, no, I was shooting out that way."

"I'm sure you didn't do it." Frank grabbed Catherine's arm to steady her, recoiling when she hissed in pain.

Vivian leaned in closer, then exclaimed, "My God, you're bleeding."

Chapter 17

Joshua gnashed his back teeth together until it felt as if his jaw had splintered. He was trying hard to rein in his temper as he followed Vivian and Nate upstairs to their borrowed suite at the Stage House. Taking a couple of deep breaths didn't help even out his anger.

While Richard and Catherine got their injuries attended to over at Doc Sheaton's office, Harrison settled his family into a room at Maude's boardinghouse for the night. Retta said it'd give her some time to visit with the widow, who'd made the decision to run the business by herself. Stubborn to the bone, that was Maude Adams.

Nobody felt like staying out at the ranches, not with Lucinda's windows and walls shot to shit and spots of blood on the ground. Joshua hoped it was the gunman's blood and not just Richard's. Once Nate's pup and Addie's dog had been secured inside Harrison's stable with the horses, everyone had headed for town.

Frank had been in high form, raging over Catherine being wounded, though it'd been little more than a graze. Some alcohol and a padded bandage had helped ease her pain. Richard's injury was found to be problematic, with the bullet lodged in his thigh. Doc'd had to operate, the process delicate owing to the main leg artery, but he'd removed the bullet with minimal damage. Even so, Richard's recuperation would take at least a month.

Nate had fallen into bed without a murmur of protest, burrowing into his blankets, asleep almost before Vivian could pull the covers over his shoulders. They'd left a single lamp burning on the bureau in case he awoke in the night.

Reaching their room, Joshua silently opened the door, still too furious to speak, afraid he'd say something that would damage the new understanding he'd reached with Vivian. Truth be told, he was more angry with himself than her. He'd been a fool to allow her to talk him into leaving her and the Carter women alone for the night, when everyone suspected danger lurked nearby.

With my wife the possible target.

No, that mistake wouldn't happen again. If Richard hadn't been there to protect them, much worse could have happened.

As she moved past him, still wearing her pretty flowered dressing gown, her soft womanly scent swamped his senses. Desire and a strong dose of protectiveness tore through him, along with irritation at himself that he'd rushed her and Nate from the ranch without even allowing either of them five minutes to put on proper clothes. Getting them out of that mess had been the most important thing.

His brows snapped down. Vivian's ability to roam freely had come to an end. Nate, too. From this point forward, if he wasn't by her side when in town, one of his deputies would be. And he'd bet money Catherine and Retta would find their activities curtailed as well.

"Are you sure Richard is going to be all right?" Vivian asked, twisting her hands together as she perched on the edge of the bed. The bluish shadows beneath her eyes strengthened his resolve to do better at keeping her safe.

Forcing his shoulders to relax, he took a seat next to her. "Doc said the bullet came out in one piece, didn't hit the bone. He'll be fine." Joshua cupped the side of her face, sliding his thumb across her cheek. "But that's twice your life has been in danger."

Her eyes blurred with emotion. "He was hurt because of me."

"No," Joshua growled, "don't even think that for a moment."

When two fat tears overflowed, he tugged her up against his chest. Vivian slipped her arms around his waist and rested her head over his heart, sobbing softly.

Joshua dropped a kiss against her silky hair, a sense of helplessness blanketing him. He didn't know how to comfort a crying woman.

"Shh," he murmured, rocking her gently. "If it's anybody's fault, it's mine. I should never have left you unprotected like that."

Lifting up a tearstained face, a wobbly smile curved her lips. "Aren't we the pair, both blaming ourselves for another's evil actions. And with no idea who lurked out there, shooting in the first place." She rubbed at her damp cheek. "At least Nate was with you and my brothers."

She straightened, and Joshua reluctantly released her, fighting the desire thrumming through him. The need to take Vivian back into his arms and make love to her, battled with his decision to take it slow.

I'm a selfish ass. She was traumatized by the evening's events and all he could think about was getting her back into his bed.

He'd almost lost her twice now. At the moment his emotions were too unstable, his ability to concentrate on the bastard who opened fire on a houseful of innocent women just as scattered. The need to claim her again, to cherish her, was like a livable breathing force inside him. *Not tonight.* Tenderness was not what he was feeling at the moment, only fury over the danger she'd been in, and possessiveness. Lust.

So much lust.

Joshua wanted to strip her naked and join with her again, to make her his in every way possible. Images of doing just that flashed across his mind, and a growl rumbled in his chest.

Vivian's eyes widened, and he silently chastised himself for frightening her.

"Why don't you get some sleep?" He started to rise. "I'll stand guard tonight."

She placed a staying hand on his chest.

"No." She cleared her throat, using her other hand to wipe away the remnants of her tears. "Lie with me again, as man and wife."

Her words were brave, but the blush that rose to her cheeks gave away her anxiousness. A wave of affection for his adorable wife rose swiftly within him.

She deserves so much better than me.

As if sensing his hesitation, she offered a smile that stirred his body.

"I want you, Joshua."

The softly spoken words only made him more determined to do what was right. He'd hurt her last time, and until he could control himself to assure it didn't happen again, he planned to keep his hands off her.

~ ~ ~

Vivian's nerves rioted like butterflies, even as her heart raced with excitement. Tonight, she wanted to feel the touch of this man again. *My husband.* Strong, brave, oh so handsome, she'd been smitten with Joshua Lang from the moment she'd looked into his thick-lashed hazel eyes and heard her name fall from his lips.

He abruptly stood, and her stomach sank in dismay. Denial shone plainly on his face. She knew he thought of her as too young, too sheltered to be married to a rough lawman, but he was wrong. Growing up, she'd possessed an avid curiosity about life and what it had to offer. That eagerness had only gotten stronger as she'd matured. She'd never be satisfied to just sit back as the world and all its wonders passed her by, while men and circumstances dictated her actions.

Before she'd met her amazing sisters-by-marriage, Vivian had longed to break free of her social confinements. Now, she was even more resolute. She'd never been more thrilled than when her mama finally agreed to follow Frank and Harrison out West.

Time to be brave.

Time to do all in her power to banish from her husband's mind the danger this evening had already wrought. It was over and she was safe. Nothing else mattered but rediscovering the intimacy of their marriage. Tasting such passion once, she wanted it again.

Now, before he put up any more barriers between them.

Rising, she untied her robe. The soft cotton parted as the sleeves slid down her arms. She pushed the garment to the floor, leaving her wearing nothing but her smocked nightgown. Bolstering her courage, she whipped the thin batiste over her head and flung it away.

The look on Joshua's face, as he perused her bared flesh, sent a surge of satisfaction through her.

Take that, husband, she thought smugly. She wasn't the helpless little miss he perceived her to be. And if he thought she was put off by his past, he was wrong.

His eyes darkened the same way they had the first time he'd seen her naked.

Vivian swayed closer and settled her hands on his chest. The muscles under her palms rippled and bunched beneath the fabric of his shirt in the most interesting ways. When she brushed her thumbs over his flat, male nipples, he sucked in a sharp breath.

The ache between her thighs deepened, making her yearn to feel him moving inside her again.

"What are you doing, angel?"

She barely recognized his voice, all low and rumbly. Her trepidation disappeared. Vivian loved this man, trusted him with her body and her life. They were meant to be together. This Vivian knew, just as she knew the grass was green and the plains dusty.

In time, he'll love me back.

"I don't know what I'm doing, Joshua," she admitted. Tugging his shirt from his pants, she peeked up at him from under her lashes. "Can you show me?"

She tucked her hands under the loose material, gripping his sides just above the waistband of his trousers.

Tenderness softened his gaze. "What makes you think I know what I'm doing?"

"What do you mean?"

"I . . ." Joshua paused, clearly trying to collect himself, then grasped her hands, bringing them up to kiss first one palm, then the other. "There are things about me you still don't know, and maybe you should."

Reclaiming his seat on the bed, he gathered her close. His warmth enveloped her, but the cool air on her bare back sent a shiver through her. He grasped the quilt from the foot of the bed and brought it around her shoulders. "Better?"

She nodded, staring into his eyes so he could read her sincerity. "Nothing you can say will make me change the way I feel about you. I love you, Joshua Lang, and that'll always remain constant."

~ ~ ~

Everything inside Joshua stilled at her vow. It wasn't possible this precious woman loved him. How could she, when she didn't really know him? He'd hidden his sordid past from everyone. It wasn't only his early years at the bordello that shamed him, there were other things . . .

She needs to know it all.

He tucked her head beneath his chin, tightening his arms around her. At least this way he wouldn't see the condemnation in her eyes.

"You know I was born in a whorehouse." At her soft murmur he continued, "It's all right, angel. I was glad to get it all off my chest that day. Glad your brothers heard it, too. And I made peace with my upbringing long ago. But living in a place like that changes a boy."

"Tell me, please."

Joshua took a moment to gather his thoughts. "I told you my ma was a whore. Her meanness and her drinking got her killed by one of her customers. After she died, I had nowhere to go. One of the whores took pity on me and taught me to read and write. It was the only book learnin' I got. When I was old enough to think for myself, I left. Bounced around a little, took odd jobs when I could find them. Gambled a bit, drank some, things a stupid kid still wet behind the ears might do. Eventually I joined the Texas Rangers."

"How old were you by then?"

Almost fifteen. I was tall and husky for my age. Lied and said I was eighteen. Nobody questioned me." He stroked her hair, finding the action soothed him. "I aligned myself alongside the Rangers in the name of the law. Meted out justice when I was told to. Stayed long enough to understand like anything else in this world, there's good and bad. I met some wonderful Kiowa families when I recommissioned in the Rangers. Kind, proud folk. Then found myself disillusioned when the oath I spoke to obtain my star also meant I had to fight the very people who had befriended me in the first place."

He fell silent, the memories overtaking him as if it'd all happened yesterday instead of years ago.

Vivian stroked the back of his neck. "That's not all, is it?"

"No," he admitted, thinking what came next would be hardest to share. "There was an older Ranger, one of the underlings but still above most of the recommissioned men. Some of us found out he'd been encouraging atrocities against the Indians and Mexicans we fought. Against the women and children. I know war is war, but what he let happen was dishonorable to the Ranger code. Even in violent times there has to be honor in why a war is fought in the first place. When I tried to bring his actions to light, I was told all was fair in battle."

Joshua nestled his wife closer, needing her warmth, her compassion. "I couldn't stay any longer. I hadn't the thirst for the level of violence I saw in some of the men. I turned in my star and chose to travel for a while. Eventually I headed for the silver mines like a lot of young men did. Found myself in Little Creede right about the time when the town needed a lawman." Firming his lips, he waited for her to ask the tougher questions he wasn't willing to answer.

For several long moments she didn't say anything but remained close to his side, her arms around his waist. He felt her sigh as she raised her face to his and met his hooded gaze, compassion in her eyes. "Joshua, your past, both childhood and young adulthood, was awful but that doesn't make you less in my opinion. You got away, you did good things with your life. Which is admirable to say the least."

Joshua straightened and set her from him gently, holding her by the shoulders when she tried to inch closer. "Angel, my past is nothing to be proud of. It's made me rough and inflexible at the best of times."

Vivian tenderly cupped his jaw. "It almost sounds as if you're wanting to be judged, and if that's so, then let me make up my own mind. It's only fair."

With a shake of his head, Joshua gave in to the blinding need to hold her. "Not yet, angel. Right now I want to show you tenderness. I want to savor and cherish you."

"But—"

Cutting off her words, he bent and covered her mouth with his. As she melted under his passionate kiss, he silently vowed she'd never know anything but magic in his lovemaking.

~ ~ ~

Vivian's pulse raced, her body tingling the same way it had the first time they'd lain together. Recalling that moment, she found herself eager to experience again the feel of his hard flesh against her most intimate spot.

A small moan escaped her and vibrated against his lips.

Joshua eased her back onto the bed and into the mussed sheets. At the way his smoldering stare took her in from head to curling toes, a hot flush scalded her skin. Which only grew hotter when he trailed a hand up the inside of her leg to just under her knee.

Suddenly feeling inordinately shy, she lifted her hands to cover her breasts, but stopped halfway when he said quietly, "No. Don't hide from me."

She dropped her hands back to the mattress. Joshua was her husband, and she wanted this to happen. Shyness had no place in her marriage bed.

He slid his hand up a few more inches and curled his palm around her thigh, squeezing gently. "You're the most beautiful thing I've ever seen, angel, and I thank my lucky stars that you're mine."

The sincerity in his words, the appreciation in his eyes, all worked to erase any remaining doubt in her mind. "I'm glad I'm yours, Joshua."

Their gazes locked, and Vivian had never felt closer to him than she did right then. She could almost see the emotional bond between them grow, moment by moment as time ticked along. Finally, Joshua broke the contact and quickly removed his clothes.

Her eyes lowered to his erect manhood, and she could only stare at the size. No wonder it'd hurt that first time. Even though she'd touched him there, his size was imposing to actually see. How had it ever fit inside her, to begin with?

Catherine had assured she'd only feel pleasure from this point on. But still . . .

At the sound of his husky chuckle, Vivian's gaze shot back up to his face as he climbed onto the bed and covered her completely. She loved the feel of him pressing her into the mattress with his muscled frame, his intoxicating male scent surrounding her.

"I'll be gentle," he promised, sliding one hand under her hair and cupping her nape. His mouth lowered to hers in a slow, languid kiss, as if they had all the time in the world.

Vivian lost herself to the feel of his lips moving over hers, their tongues entwining together. Any doubt or anxiousness disappeared, leaving only desire.

Slipping a hand between them, Joshua cupped her breast, his thumb stroking her nipple until it grew taut with need, then repeating the action with her other breast as it too throbbed beneath his touch.

Vivian moaned at the sensation of his large palms against her skin, intensifying the ache to be filled by him. "Joshua . . ." Instinctively, her legs parted in silent invitation. She clutched his shoulders, moving restlessly beneath him.

"Easy," he murmured, even as his hand trailed to her sensitive core with the gentlest of touches. "There's no rush, angel. We have all night."

"All night," she echoed. "Yes, please."

Chapter 18

Looking out from her makeshift desk in the temporary schoolroom, Vivian counted heads. Eleven of varying hair colors, some combed, others braided or in pigtails. A few tousled and tangled.

One, missing. She counted again. Eleven instead of twelve, and Nate's black curls nowhere to be seen.

"Where's Nate?" she asked the children at large. Several sets of wide eyes looked up at her question, though no one answered. Blowing out a sigh, Vivian turned to Jubal Washburn, Clem and Nellie's youngest boy. "Jubal? Where did Nate run off to? Weren't you with him earlier?"

Jubal shook his head so hard, his gingery locks flopped in his eyes. "Just to say 'hey,' Missus Vivian. When me and the others came in." He nodded toward his sisters and brothers, clumped together at one of the back tables. "Rosie, you seen Nate?"

Rose glanced up from the cat-and-cradle game she played with older sister Lizzie. "Huh?" At Vivian's raised brows, she hastily stood. "Sorry, ma'am, um, Missus Vivian, I'll put it away."

"No, you ninny," Jubal retorted. "Teacher wants to know where Nate is." His freckled face showed brotherly exasperation.

"Nate? I ain't seen him. And don't call me a ninny. Or I'll punch you in the nose." She doubled her fists. "I'm older than you and I can lick you fair and square."

As the remaining Washburn brood jumped to their feet

and started noisily taking sides, Vivian clapped her hands sharply. "All right, everyone. Settle down." She pointed at each sibling in turn. "You can bicker all you want once you get out of class, but no bloodshed in here. John," she addressed the sixteen-year-old, a spitting image of his father, Clem, "settle your kin, all right?"

"Yes, Missus Vivian." As the other children snickered, John adopted an intimidating pose, until his brothers and sisters subsided in their seats, with some grumbling and a few sticking out their tongues at each other. John sent them all a final glare, before taking his own seat.

Vivian tamped down a smile at the feisty bunch. Nellie and Clem had their hands full.

So do I if I can't find that rascal of mine before class starts.

No sooner had she thought it than she realized she already considered Nate her own son. Moisture gathered in her eyes and she had to blink several times to clear them. Hard on the heels of emotion, came concern. It wasn't like Nate to disappear right before school began.

She turned to Levi Barnes, the oldest at seventeen and one of the most studious. "Levi, please pass out the slates and lead the class in their sevens. I'll be right back." She waited until Levi trooped to the back table and gathered up slates and chalk, before heading to the kitchens. Nate might have gone over to the mercantile for a morning cookie, though he knew better than to run off somewhere by himself right now.

Especially now.

In the kitchen Mary stood at the kneading block and industriously shaped loaves of bread dough, while Trudy plucked feathers from a fat, headless chicken. Holding a hand over her midriff at the sight of the blood-streaked bird, Vivian swallowed sudden nausea, clearing her throat. "Ladies, have either of you seen Nate?"

"Yep," Mary replied. She set the blob of dough aside, wiping her hands on her apron. "I sent him to Betsey's with the hand-wagon for today's desserts, oh, maybe half an hour ago. Told him to be back fast in time for schoolin'." A frown creased her wrinkled face. "My goodness, he's been gone a bit, hasn't he?" Her cheeks suddenly lost all color. "Oh, no, I didn't even think . . . the trouble you had just lately . . ." She clapped a hand over her mouth and collapsed onto the closest chair.

With a rapidly sinking stomach, Vivian made for the rear service door. "Trudy, please sit in class for me." Not waiting for an answer, she hurried from the back-porch stoop and took the worn path that wound between and behind buildings. With each step her heart pounded harder and guilt assuaged her for failing to emphasize to the rest of the staff the importance of not sending Nate off—alone—on any errands. Of course, Ben and a few other men in town were patrolling regularly, but she knew full well how easy it was for a youngster to take the back trails and become lost in the taller brush.

She wasn't about to relax her guard or her vigilance. Not until she knew for certain Florence Johnson was gone from here. Not until Joshua had caught whoever came onto Carter land and started shooting.

Nate, the first one in the schoolroom no matter the distraction, was always eager to help out. But even a chore like fetching for the kitchen staff wouldn't detain him for long, and Betsey would know better than to hold him up.

Vivian rounded the edge of the mercantile where the supply shed met the path, sick with worry.

At the sight of the overturned hand-wagon, she gave a sharp cry. Betsey's pies and tarts, a few of her cakes, spilled out over the dirt. Wildly, Vivian pivoted, squinting in the sun, fright making her breath hitch and stall in her lungs.

"Oh, Lord, please. Please," she muttered under her breath as she dashed toward Betsey's back door.

~ ~ ~

Joshua jammed the *Wanted* poster on one of the nails embedded in the wall. Standing back to adjust the thick piece of paper, he took due note of the bearded face and hard sneer of the latest fugitive from justice. Although Territorial sent these posters out only once a year or so, chances were good this particular criminal—as well as the three others decorating the jail office wall—would remain 'wanted' for a long time. Armed and dangerous, these men could be anywhere.

Though Ben Parsons had become a sturdy, dependable right-hand man for the jail and a damned good deputy, the town needed more policing, and not merely the occasional posse hastily gathered when trouble reared its head. Even after Richard came back on duty, it wouldn't be enough especially when the mines and outlying areas required protection, too.

Joshua had reached for a second poster on his desk, when a commotion outside got his attention. Frowning, he rose and headed to the window, spotting Vivian running down the street toward the jail, Betsey Loman hurrying to keep up. Ben, worry written all over his face, brought up the rear.

Joshua grabbed his holster and wrenched open the door. He'd been at his desk less than an hour.

What the hell could have happened in an hour?

He strode onto the porch, meeting his wife halfway up the steps, and tossed the holster over one arm, catching her as she flung herself against him.

"Angel, what's wrong?" He eased back, holding her shoulders, feeling how she trembled under his palms. Her eyes were bright with unshed tears, her face pinched.

"Nate's missing. He's *missing*, Joshua. I found—I found—" She gulped, clutching the front of his shirt. "The wagon. You have to find him, the wagon's all spilled and there was a scuffle in the dirt . . ."

His gut twisted with worry. "Missing? What wagon?"

Vivian burrowed into his shoulder, sagging against him. "What if that woman took him this time?"

Forcing down his own panic, Joshua held her close, and faced Betsey as she stumbled to a stop on the bottom step, a hand fisted over her heart. "Betsey?"

"He came to get the desserts and such. Had the little wagon with him." Betsey sucked in a shaky breath. "I loaded it up for him and off he went with that big grin of his, happy as can be. I never saw or heard a thing, I swear." Her free hand twisted in the folds of her apron. "If only I'd gone with him."

Ben had reached the porch. "Sheriff, I was outside the front of the mercantile when Vivian ran in." He paused, blotting his sweaty forehead with his sleeve. "I started asking around right away. Turns out Jaworski saw Nate with some cowpoke. Jack didn't recognize him. Figured it was one of the miners who spends off-season on the range beyond Silver Cache."

Vivian went even whiter. "Nate wouldn't go off with someone without telling me." She tightened her grip on Joshua's shirt until her nails dug into his chest. "Joshua, we have to find him."

"Don't worry, we'll get him." Joshua set Vivian aside gently and buckled his holster around his hips. "Go with Betsey. Find Frank and let him know. Then I want you to stay with Catherine."

"*No*." Vivian dashed away tears. "I'm going with you. I need to find our boy."

"Vivian, listen now." Joshua took her by the shoulders

and stared into her anguished eyes. "I can't be worrying about you while I'm hunting for Nate. Use your head, woman."

He tried to pull her toward Betsey, but Vivian dug in her heels and refused to budge. Joshua released her and tried a different tactic. If anything happened to her, he'd go mad. "You need to stay with the other children."

"The other children are fine. They're all *safe*. I need to find Nate, and I'm either going with you or I'll search for him on my own." She whirled toward the steps.

"Jesus save me." Annoyed past reason, Joshua grabbed her sleeve. "Are you crazy? You're not going off on your own."

"I'm a worried mother and I'm scared to death." She shook off his hand. "Are you going to let me come with you?"

He resisted pulling his hair out in frustration, and instead finished tying his holster straps to his legs, forcing himself to calm down, before straightening and glaring at the stubborn woman he'd married. "No."

"Joshua—"

All his calm fled as he snatched her to his chest and bent her backward, taking her lips in a kiss that tasted as desperate as he felt. Breaking away, he lifted her right off her feet until she dangled before him with a gaping mouth and widened eyes. "I will not chance something happening to you, and I can't do what needs to be done if I'm worried about your safety. So do what I say."

He set her down carefully, retaining hold of her hands. "Please help me by staying with Catherine. Or Retta."

Her shoulders slumped as she let out a sigh. "All right."

Relieved she had agreed to do as he asked, Joshua leaned down to give her a final kiss, before releasing her to Betsey's solicitous mothering. The older woman led Vivian down the boardwalk toward the Stage House.

How thankful he was for the caring souls who lived in their little town. If asked, they'd do anything for each other.

"Oh, little girl, I know all of the Lucky Lady's secrets." Florence jabbed the gun muzzle harder. "Including Slim's hidden door and the passageway that runs through the building."

~ ~ ~

Frustration, anger, and fear all coiled inside Joshua like a snake about to strike. There'd been no sign of Nate. Even with Frank's outstanding tracking skills, they hadn't been able to locate the boy. The dust storm that'd rolled in obscured their vision and would undoubtably destroy any tracks they could follow. Dismounting in front of the jailhouse, he grimly faced the search party.

Frank strode toward him. "We won't stop looking until we find your boy."

Harrison joined them. "Nate's family now, Joshua. Nothing'll keep us from bringing him home."

Joshua nodded, warmth helping to settle him. Growing up as he had without any real folks—no brothers or sisters, either—this kind of acceptance from the Carters had gifted him life's best prize. A cherished wife. A strong, kind son. A decent and caring family, the likes of which he'd never dreamed possible for himself.

Fresh determination strengthened him. They would find Nate and bring him back to Vivian. Failure was unacceptable. "Damn straight we will." He directed his attention to the rest of the men. "Get some grub and some rest. Meet me back here as soon as the storm passes."

They still had a full afternoon before them to search, and Joshua wasn't going to waste a minute of it. While Harrison headed over to the boardinghouse to check on Retta and Maude, Joshua walked with Frank toward the Stage House.

"How's Vivian doing?" Frank asked.

"She's having a difficult time. Barely sleeps. If anything

happens to that boy . . ." Joshua couldn't even say the words, as his gut tightened.

"He's a tough kid." Frank's words came out gruff, as if his throat was clogged. "Remember how he took a bullet for Vivian last year?"

"Yeah." Joshua still recalled the way his heart had stilled to see Vivian and Nate hit the ground, blood flying, not knowing which one had been shot, or how bad. It'd been the longest minutes of his life before the gunfire stopped and he could find out. "I remember. He's still just a young'un, Frank, no matter how brave." Now it was Joshua's turn to choke up. "He may not be my blood, but he's my son."

"I know. Hell, the whole town knows that." As they entered the Stage House Frank gave him a hard slap on the back that made him stumble, something the man did far too often. "Get some rest yourself, Sheriff. Storm shouldn't last more than an hour."

While Frank strode off in search of Catherine, Joshua sprinted up the stairs, anxious to see his wife, hold her in his arms. Offer her the comfort he knew she'd need, since he'd come home without Nate.

Again.

She wasn't in their room, so he went back downstairs to the salon currently used for school but found it empty.

Hearing Catherine's low murmur from the main parlor, he made his way back down the hall. Inside, Frank sat near the bar, Catherine cuddled close. Joshua's gaze swept the room, but he didn't see Vivian. He scowled. Where the hell was she?

Frank set his wife aside and got to his feet. "What's wrong?"

Joshua sought out Catherine. "Have you seen Vivian?"

"Yes, she was feeling ill, so she went upstairs for a nap."

"What? She was fine this morning." His eyes narrowed

at the way Catherine glanced away, a sure sign of deception. "Where's my wife, Catherine?"

"I told you, she's laying down."

"Cat," Frank murmured. "What are you girls up to?"

"Nothing. She's got to be here somewhere."

"She's not in our room." Joshua strode into the kitchen, Frank and Catherine hot on his heels. Not finding Vivian there, he hurriedly checked the rest of the Stage House, avoiding the private rooms where he knew his wife wouldn't go.

Worry gnawing in his stomach like a pack of starving rats, he rushed back upstairs to see if she'd returned.

The suite was still empty.

As Catherine and Frank crowded in the doorway, Joshua snapped, "Tell me what's going on, Catherine."

"Don't talk to my wife that way, Lang," Frank growled, though he turned to her with a frown. "Spill, darlin'. I know you're not telling us everything."

As she hesitated, he softened his voice. "Cat, please."

The seriousness of her husband's demand must have finally gotten through, because Catherine's face blanched of color. "She's truly not here?" She grabbed Joshua's sleeve. "What if she tried to go after Nate herself? You have to find her. Doc Sheaton thinks she's carrying your child."

Chapter 20

After bouncing face-down on the back of a horse for what felt like hours, Vivian was roughly yanked off, then pushed and pulled over the ground as she struggled to stay on her feet. Her bleary gaze took in a broken-down miner's cabin.

Florence shoved her through the open door. "Say hello to Slim Morgan, little girl."

Vivian landed on the floor in front of a pair of scuffed, muddy boots.

Though she'd been told the man was alive, she gaped at the sight of Slim Morgan. Appearing older than she'd expected, the scarring on his face added to his sinister visage. He stank of whisky and sweat.

Vivian shrank back and sucked in deep gulps of air, desperately trying to control her urge to vomit. When he loomed over her, one side of his thin mouth curling mockingly, she lost the battle, and, gagging, purged what little remained in her stomach. The sour stench of vomit caused her to heave again, until her throat was on fire.

From the corner of her eye she saw his boot sidestep the mess she'd produced. His curses turned the air blue, before he snarled, "Flo, get that puking bitch out of here."

His boot reared back threateningly as Vivian moaned and curled into a protective ball.

Then she heard Nate shout, "Leave her alone, Morgan!"

Her relief at knowing Nate was alive was tempered with fear as Slim pivoted from where she lay.

"What did you call me?" Slim advanced threateningly. Only a few feet away and glaring in fury, Nate didn't yield an inch despite how frightened he must be. "I'm your father, and you'll show some respect. Now get the rope, you're going back into the mine."

"I *said* I ain't going back in."

"You'll do what I say." Slim lunged clumsily, one of his legs twisted, oddly off-balance, and Nate scuttled sideways, avoiding the man's attempts to grab him.

Crouching next to Vivian, Nate used his body as a shield. Through teary eyes she could see the way his thin arms trembled as he held them out on either side of her. For a few precious seconds her boy remained close enough for her to rub his back and, she hoped, reassure with her touch.

Until with a snarl Florence ripped him away.

"You obey your pa, you little no-account." She pushed him hard and he stumbled, Morgan catching him by the neck. "Ungrateful brat." Florence spun to confront Vivian. "And you, thinking you can take my child."

She hauled back with one arm and swung. Her open palm connected hard with Vivian's cheek, once. Then again. As Vivian's head snapped back, the woman dragged her across the rough floor, muttering under her breath.

Amidst Nate's cries and Slim's cruel laughter, Vivian felt herself sinking, her face throbbing, darkness encroaching on her numbed brain, her body bumping over dirt and scrub as Florence Johnson yanked her from the cabin.

~ ~ ~

With a sharp nod, Harrison raised his palm from the Bible Joshua held. Newly sworn in as a deputy, he'd repeated the oath alongside Frank, both brothers promising to uphold the law and administer fair justice.

Joshua set the Bible on his desk, gripping the worn leather briefly, pulling what strength he could from his own well of faith. Frank's hand on his shoulder brought his attention around, and he met the man's hard stare.

"We're gonna find them," Frank assured gruffly.

"Yeah, we are." Joshua swept up his hat and dropped it into place, then adjusted the double holster already buckled around his hips. "Let's go." He strode to the door, collecting his repeater as he stepped outside.

Fearing that Vivian's disappearance was a direct result of Nate's abduction, Joshua had searched for a physical link between the two. The only name he could come up with was Florence Johnson, though why she would have taken Vivian, he hadn't a clue. But for now, the former Lucky Lady whore was his prime suspect.

A gut feeling also told him everything was connected to the shootout at the ranch, too.

Ike Barnes would meet them at the edge of town, and they'd ride for the lower Cascades where several abandoned cabins might provide hiding places. Joshua had sent Robert and Ben to Silver Cache on the off-chance Florence had headed in that direction. Retta had persuaded Maude Adams to join the others at the Stage House, with Dub providing support for Lucinda and pairing up with Silas to guard the rest of the women and the Carter children. Several men and a few miners, all armed, patrolled the town.

Until they knew all of what they were up against, Joshua had no choice but to assume the very worst. With the way the menfolk rallied, treating this situation with the seriousness it deserved, he could center his worry where it belonged, on finding Vivian and Nate.

As they saddle-sheathed their rifles and untethered their horses, shouts and commotion spun Joshua toward the eastern section of town where the Gambling Galleria was located.

"Sheriff, hold up."

Striding along the sidewalk, silver conchos jangling with each clomp of his boots, Knight Gleason bore down, one beefy hand clutching the arm of a struggling figure. As they drew closer, Joshua's eyes narrowed, recognizing the swine who'd put his filthy paws on Vivian.

Harrison turned and squinted. "That who I think it is?"

Frank growled low in his throat. "Yep."

Gleason frog-marched Doo Spivey so hard and fast, the man's feet tripped over each other. Squirming in an attempt to get away, the skinny fool was no match for the massive Galleria owner.

"Looky what ah got heah, boys." Gleason shook Spivey like a rat, forcing a whine from the man's scrawny gullet. "Caught the lil' pissant tryin' to break in mah desk. Nuthin' in theah but vouchers." He shook Spivey again. "Yew wanna lock this idjit up afore ah decide to choke him by his chicken neck?"

Spivey stiffened in Gleason's grip, bug-eyed. "You can't do that."

Joshua drew his right-hand Colt from its holster and positioned the muzzle under Spivey's chin. "He can't, but I can."

Spivey's Adam's apple rippled as he swallowed. "I ain't done nuthin' but come back to town."

"Sheriff Lang told you what would happen if you ever showed yourself around here again," Frank bit out, crowding Spivey on the right while Harrison bunched both fists and took up the left. With Gleason behind him and Joshua's Colt still pressing in, the cur had nowhere to go. "You must have a powerful need to die today, Spivey. I don't know why the hell you came back, but if you got a ready excuse, better start talking. *Now.*"

When Spivey flattened his lips and said nothing, Joshua jammed the muzzle harder. "I don't have time for this, you asshole." He nodded toward the jail, and then Gleason.

"You're hereby deputized, Mister Gleason. Lock him up. If he happens to slip on the floor and get his face banged up or a kneecap blown out, well, that's too bad. He can rot in there until Territorial sends out the wagon for him."

"Ah'd be right proud to, Sheriff."

As Gleason grasped hold of the back of Spivey's neck, the craven piece of dung screeched, "No prison, I'll tell you anythin' you wanna know."

"Gonna make it worth my while?" Joshua cocked the hammer, its click loud in the still air.

Spivey gulped and blubbered, "I know where Slim Morgan is. Flo Johnson, too. I can take you right to them."

"Morgan? That bastard is dead. How the hell are you connected to a dead man?" As Joshua gaped at hearing verification that a criminal they'd thought long-gone still lived, Spivey nodded so frantically, he came close to impaling his throat on Joshua's gun.

"I'll show you. I'm not lyin', neither, he's alive. Found him myself, down off the rapids where that creek splits off. I'll tell you everythin', just don't lock me up. I already been to prison once and I can't go back." Spivey hung in Gleason's fist, the toes of his battered boots dragging in the dust.

Joshua considered the weasel. "You know anything about shooting up a ranch that belongs to my wife's family?" He played with the Colt's cocked hammer, grimly noting the way sweat dripped off the man's forehead and his skin took on a gray tinge as he finally accepted how close to death he was about to come.

Seconds passed, until with a snarl, Joshua turned away. "He's all yours, Gleason."

"No! I did it, all right? I confess." Spivey's entire body sagged as if all the air had left him. "Flo Johnson said she'd pay me in silver."

~ ~ ~

Vivian's eyes fluttered, then opened, blurry and aching. The thick smell of dust-ore surrounded her and nausea rose swiftly up her throat. Staring at an uneven rock ceiling, she took deep shallow breaths, until the feeling passed. She slowly sat up and glanced around, thankful for the single candle attached to a rusted sconce that at least provided minimal light.

Where's Nate?

She breathed a sigh of relief when she spotted him sitting several feet away, tied to a nail embedded in what appeared to be a shaft support, his small hands bound by rope.

Comprehension blended with horror when her focus sharpened. They were imprisoned in the mine, the walls bracketed with ancient-looking wooden planks. A pull on her wrists confirmed she was tied up and attached to a wall bracket as well, though some slack had been added to the rope which allowed her to move about a little.

A dirty cotton tarpaulin covered most of the mine opening. A split in the stiff cloth showed the brightness of a full moon outside. Inside, the air smelled fetid from tallow smoke. Vivian straightened, her muscles protesting with each movement, until she could prop herself against a log.

She squinted, making out a darkened corridor, with stones occasionally tumbling down over oilcloth shredded from too much stress. Their safety was surely in peril.

"Nate?" she whispered urgently.

In the dimness she saw him start at the sound of her voice and struggle to his knees. "I'm here, Missus Vivian."

The sound of his sweet young voice, trying so hard to be brave, brought stinging tears to her eyes and Vivian blinked furiously to stave them off. "Can you get loose?"

"I don't know."

"We have to try." She could hear Slim's muffled voice but couldn't understand what he was saying. "How far are we from the cabin?"

"Maybe twenty yards."

"How long have we been here?"

"It's pretty dark outside. An hour, I'm guessin'." His breath hitched. "You were so still, I was afraid . . ."

"I'm all right," she reassured him. "But we need to get away. Do you know when they'll sleep?"

"A while yet. They'll start drinking first. Always do." Nate coughed and wiped his nose on his shirt. His gaze, far too adult for such a young boy, met hers. "Then they'll fornicate, before they start snoring." His mouth pinched tight. "Same thing every night."

She felt sick at the imagery his comment produced. "Oh, darling." Then her insides actually did pinch, and two seconds later she was leaning over to vomit again. Her heaving didn't last long this time since she had nothing in her stomach, but it left her feeling even weaker.

"Missus Vivian?"

Struggling to regain some strength, she straightened. "I feel better, truly," she lied. "I know it's not pleasant having to deal with someone who's throwing up."

He shrugged. "Living in the saloon, you get to see things like that. Mostly when folks drink too much." His matter-of-fact, too-adult response broke her heart. "Anyway, as soon as it's light enough in the morning they'll prob'ly send me into the mine again to dig out the ore. The first time, they tied a rope around me so's they could tug me back, but the tunnel's thin. I got stuck and started coughing something terrible." His voice petered out to a rasp. "I don't want to go back in. If I die in there, what'll become of you?"

"Oh, sweet boy." No longer able to hold back her tears, they flowed hotly down her cheeks. "By now the town must know we're missing. Joshua will find us, you have to believe—"

"This mine is mighty hard to spot. I saw for myself," Nate broke in. "But I kind of know whereabouts we are.

There's caves above us and the hills go on forever." He was silent a moment. "If we could get free, I could maybe hide you in the caves and go get help."

"I'm not letting you run off by yourself."

"You have to. Because you're gonna have a babe. Aren't you?"

She gasped. "How would you know that?"

"I know what it means when a lady throws up the way you did. 'Cept none of them at the saloon were ladies. Not like you," he added.

"Nate . . ."

"You can't run around out there like I can. You're too sick. I'll find a safe place for you and you can hide there while I get Sheriff Joshua."

For a long while the silence was broken by the sputter of the tallow candle, and the rustling of clothing as they tried to settle as comfortably as their restraints allowed. Vivian dozed a few times, waking to cough, her queasy stomach forcing a few dry heaves.

"We got water, Missus Vivian. They dropped a canteen over here. Once we get loose I'll bring it to you." He nodded toward a dented tin container within reach of his bound hands.

"Well, that's something in our favor." She licked her dry lips, recoiling at the lingering taste of bile. "We'll save what we can, all right?"

"Yes, ma'am." He broke off, cocking his head. "Listen. You hear that?"

Vivian strained to hear anything past the occasional coyote, then her ears picked up the sound of grunts. A moan.

A high-pitched giggle that trailed into an even louder moan.

"They'll do that for a long time," Nate stated matter-of-factly. "If we're gonna get loose, we should do it now."

"Don't hurt yourself," she cautioned, but he'd already begun pulling on his restraints, the strain showing on his face as the rope cut into his wrists. Seconds grew into minutes as he tugged, until with a groan of pain and a final yank, the old nail his rope had been tied to bent and gave way from the rotten wood.

Chapter 21

Vivian choked back tears as Nate pressed against her side. With her wrists still bound and attached to a nail, she couldn't hug him as she so desperately needed to, but the way he embraced her, holding on tightly, warmed her straight through. When she felt his thin frame shudder, a fierce urge to protect him overtook her fear. "Shh . . . I promise, it's going to be all right."

A promise she hoped to keep, even as nausea continued to roil inside her and a terrible headache throbbed behind her eyes. From morning sickness or stress and lack of food, she didn't know. Whatever caused it, she'd never be able to make the long journey back to town.

As much as she hated to admit it, Nate was right. She'd need to find a place to hide while he left on his own. If she slowed them down and Slim Morgan caught up to them, there was a good chance the man would kill them both.

The noise from the cabin had ceased at least an hour earlier, indicating its occupants finally succumbed to their inebriation. She laid her cheek briefly on his head. "Nate, we need to go."

Fresh trembles shook him, before he pulled away. She wanted to cry at the damage that awful man had done to the poor boy's face, now blotched with bruises. If she had a gun, she'd have gone in and killed the bastard.

Perhaps sensing her emotions, Nate straightened, a calmness descending over him that belied his young age. It was as if he'd matured right before her eyes. He nodded, glancing around the mine. "You're right."

He rushed over and picked up a large stone, bringing it back, pounding at the rope knots binding her wrists until they loosened from the nail and he could free her. Carefully, he helped her to her feet.

Shaking out her numbed fingers, Vivian grabbed up the canteen. "Ready?"

Nate nodded, grit and determination shining in his eyes.

Ignoring her nausea as best she could, they crept toward the exit and stepped into the warm night. Thankfully they had a full moon to guide them. Tension filled the air as they passed the cabin where Florence and Slim Morgan slept, but all remained quiet except for an owl hooting nearby.

Once they were away a safe distance, Vivian asked, "How are you doing, Nate?"

She wanted to tug him back into her arms and cry with relief, but there was no time for that. They needed to find a place to hide. At the rate she was tiring, she couldn't travel much farther.

Her hand moved to her stomach, tears clouding her vision. Even though Doc Sheaton couldn't confirm she was in fact carrying Joshua's child, Vivian knew it was so. She felt the truth of it in her heart, her very soul. Fear of losing her babe nearly overwhelmed her, and she stumbled.

Nate reached for her hand, steadying her. "It'll be all right, Ma. I'll protect you."

Her heart swelled with love for her brave little boy, followed by a rush of sadness that the first time Nate called her 'Ma' was in such a frightful situation. A sob lodged in her throat, one she refused to release. There was no time to feel sorry for herself, not when they needed shelter.

She squeezed his hand. "I know you will, darling. Right now we need to find a place to hide, and figure out what we're going to do."

They couldn't stay out in the open like this without a weapon. There were all sorts of predators wandering around in the dark, especially this far up on the ridge. By the soft light of the moon, she could see rock formations in the distance. There was bound to be a cave where they could stay until morning. Then she'd have to find the courage to send Nate to safety on his own, because she'd only slow him down. His chances of surviving this were greater without her.

God willing, he'll find his way to town and bring back help.

Nate never left her side, his quiet words of encouragement giving her the strength she needed to continue. By the time they reached their destination Vivian could barely stay upright. Her headache had only worsened, and she suspected she'd suffered a concussion.

Nate spotted the cave opening first. "I'll go in and look around to make sure it's safe."

Alarmed, Vivian rushed to get between him and the cave. "No, let me."

She immediately regretted the movement when her stomach lurched, and she spun away from the opening, bending over to throw up again. Fortunately, it didn't last long this time. *Probably nothing more to throw.*

Nate patted her back and patiently waited for the bout to pass, like he'd done each time before. Only this time he didn't have to protect her from Morgan's anger over her making a mess.

Straightening, she locked her knees so she wouldn't wobble. "I'm fine now."

Before she had the chance to instruct him to wait outside while she checked the cave, he turned and dashed inside, calling over his shoulder, "I won't be long."

Vivian wanted to stop him but didn't have the energy. Instead she leaned against a large boulder and anxiously waited. By her estimate, it'd been at least two hours since they'd fled the mine. A few more hours and there'd probably be enough daylight for Nate to descend the rest of the way. Knowing Joshua, they had a posse out looking for them, but would they be searching in the right area?

Fear curdled her insides like spoiled milk. Not fear for herself, but for Nate and the fact she might die in this desolate place without ever knowing if he'd reached safety or had perished somewhere along the trail. Her hand went to her stomach, thinking of the child who might never be born.

The tears she'd been keeping at bay spilled down her cheeks, and she angrily batted them away.

I can't fall apart now. Not while my son needs me.

Stiffening her spine, she plastered on an encouraging expression as Nate returned with a wide grin on his face.

"It's safe, Ma. C'mon."

He held out his hand and she allowed him to help her inside. It was too dark to see much, but Nate seemed to know where he was going, and she was soon sitting on the stone floor with a rock wall to her back. He sank down next to her.

Wrapping an arm around him, she hauled him close to her side and pressed her cheek to the top of his head. "Get some sleep, darling, morning will be here soon."

"How are you feeling?" he asked, concern evident in his voice as he stared up at her.

Nate appeared as exhausted as she felt. Even in the dim light, there was no missing the dark circles under his eyes that matched the rest of the bruises on his face. For a moment Vivian couldn't speak as fury choked her. If anyone deserved prison, it was Florence Johnson and Slim Morgan for what they'd put this poor child through.

Shoving aside her bitter emotions to concentrate on what was important now, getting her son to safety, she dropped a kiss against his forehead. "I'm better. Now sleep."

He yawned, and Vivian held him quietly until his soft snoring indicated he'd fallen asleep. And as hard as she tried to keep her eyes open to listen for any sounds of danger, sleep soon claimed her, too.

~ ~ ~

When Vivian opened her eyes, sunrise had begun to lighten the dim cave interior, offering her the first real look of their hiding spot. Her heart stilled when she spotted how the cave ceiling slanted higher and wider in the shadowy distance. To the right lay an opening, leading into what appeared to be a passageway.

High ceilings and passageways meant possible unseen dangers. Her anxiety rose.

So did her gorge. Nate still slept in the curve of her arm. Vivian gently set him aside and scuttled a few feet away to throw up. By the time she was through Nate knelt next to her with the canteen of water.

"Being sick only lasts a few months," he promised as she rinsed the bile from her mouth. "Honest."

She forced a smile to her lips, anxious to reassure him. When had she become the child and he the adult? "Glad to hear it," she rasped through a sore throat.

Her stomach rumbled, though she didn't feel the slightest bit hungry. Which wasn't good either since she hadn't eaten anything since the pastry from yesterday, the one she'd emptied into the spittoon. "When did you eat last, Nate?"

The journey he faced was a dangerous one, and the thought of him hungry and weak before he even left for help terrified her.

"They gave me some beans right before you arrived."

She frowned. "I'm sure they know we're missing by now, you need to go." Remembering the lemon drops she often stashed in her pockets as rewards for her students, Vivian retrieved what she had. Pain dug a hole in her chest at the thought of sending this boy out alone to find his way to town, but there was no other option. She placed the candy into his palm, then handed him the canteen. "Take the water too, I'll be fine until you bring help."

"No," he said, getting to his feet. "You keep it."

Vivian shook her head. "I'll stay inside away from the sun. If you're going to make it to town, you'll need all the water. It's our only chance."

Expression tight, he studied her for a long moment, before he reluctantly acquiesced. "I promise to come back for you."

Pride warmed her. "I know you will, darling."

Nate leaned down and planted a quick kiss on her cheek, then turned and ran from the cave.

Time crawled by slowly as the sun rose in the sky, heating up the cave to uncomfortable levels. She'd thrown up twice since Nate left. Sick as she felt, she wasn't so sure how long she'd survive. Her throat was raw from retching and the inside of her mouth felt dry as a bone. Though she desperately needed water, sending Nate off with the canteen had been the right thing to do.

Vivian estimated a couple hours passed when she heard approaching footsteps, sending her heart into her throat.

A voice carried faintly inside. "The tracks lead this way."

Slim Morgan. Oh, no.

Staggering to her feet, Vivian held back a moan as her bruised body protested the movement. On tiptoes she ventured toward the opening she'd seen earlier.

"There," Slim snarled.

Vivian slipped into the dark passageway, one hand against the rock wall guiding her steps, as Florence Johnson's voice echoed inside the cave. "Looks like she got sick here."

"They can't be far."

The passageway grew narrower, barely big enough for her to sidle through. The surrounding stone pressed in on her, shredding her breathing and making it difficult for her to continue. Gritting her teeth, she forced her feet forward.

Suddenly the walls widened again, and Vivian froze. A wider passageway might mean another cave area. Or an actual cavern. In the dark she hadn't a clue which.

The echo of footsteps drew closer. Had her pursuers entered the passageway? If she lingered here and they found her, she'd be dead for sure.

Trembling, Vivian inched forward, the wall scratching her palm as she stabilized herself along the way. Feeling as though she moved like a turtle, she dared not go faster in the dark. The *plonk* of falling rocks worried her. Surely, Morgan heard the sounds and had figured out where she was. She just hoped none of those rocks fell on the path and stopped her from advancing.

Or hit her in the head until she tumbled off into the nothingness of a cavern cliff.

Morgan's voice reached her ears, tinny but filled with rage. "It's too narrow. Get in there and follow them."

"I can't fit."

The distinct echo of a hard slap rang out. "You'll do as I say. Now get your ass in there."

Florence's muffled sob almost made Vivian sympathetic. Almost.

Sweat dripped down her forehead and into her eyes, obscuring her vision. Blinking rapidly, she crept forward, until finally she rounded a kind of curve. Feeling around with her foot, she discerned the stone was wide enough for her to hide, and a natural alcove at her back encouraged her to crouch inside—and pray Florence wouldn't find her.

Chest heaving with exhaustion and fear, she struggled to remain as still as possible. The slightest of noises amplified as she listened to Florence's shoes click along the passageway, her complaints bouncing off the rocks.

After what felt like hours, Florence finally called out. "No one's here. I'm coming back." Her footsteps sped up, accompanied by Morgan's loud obscenities at being stymied.

Then all was silent.

Vivian held her position with quivering muscles, waiting out the possibility she was being tricked into revealing herself. She counted to a hundred, then two hundred, three hundred, until the worst of her tension fell away. Taking a moment to breathe deeply and settle, she began to edge back the way she'd come.

The stone floor dipped alarmingly, and in terror she realized she had turned the wrong way. Almost in slow motion Vivian felt her feet slide out from under her.

As she tumbled down a sharp slope, the sound of her panicked scream reverberated in her ears.

~ ~ ~

"Hold up," Joshua hollered, bringing Quicksilver to a halt. They'd ridden through the lower Cascades, and the horses would need a brief rest before traversing the trail to the upper ridge. Spivey had indicated the cabin lay due west from here, less than forty yards from a silver mine where they'd forced Nate to work.

Fury burned him raw at the thought of the perils awaiting a young boy in an unstable mine. And he couldn't bear to consider the dangers facing his cherished wife and their unborn child at Morgan's hands. A growl rumbled in his chest. If the man had harmed one hair on Vivian's pretty head, he'd never make it off the ridge alive.

The law be damned. I'll tear the bastard apart and feed him to the mountain lions, piece by piece.

Harrison's wide palm landed on his shoulder. "You doing all right?"

He met his brother-by-marriage's concerned frown. Harrison Carter had always been a steady man, a solid influence for his hotheaded older brother, or anyone else who had the pleasure of crossing his path. The only time he'd ever seen his friend lose his composure had been during the early months of his marriage to Retta. That'd also been the first time he'd seen Frank step up as the more calming force in the family.

Joshua nodded, shoving aside his anger, though he had more trouble ignoring the fear overtaking him for his own family's safety. "Horses need a rest. Now's the time to take a piss if you need to, boys. We head out in ten minutes."

Frank and Ike dismounted, turning their backs to relieve themselves, while Gleason strode over to stand next to him and Harrison. His usual bluster absent, the gambler said solemnly, "That lil' gal of yers has spunk, Sheriff. Ah've no doubt she'll keep yer boy safe an' handle herself right well."

Thinking of his adorably strong-willed wife, Joshua's lips twitched. "She is tenacious at times. Determined as hell, too."

Frank joined them. "I remember when she was five and disobeyed our pa just a few days before her birthday. Pa's punishment was to deny her the fancy doll he'd ordered from one of those shops back East. I'm sure he'd have given it to her sometime later, maybe for Christmas, but Vivian wanted a doll as promised. She snuck into our parents' bedroom, swiped a pair of Pa's best boot hose and his feather pillow. Took off to the carriage house with a hank of twine and Ma's fabric shears and tried to make a doll. Brought it to the supper table that night, proud as could be." He chuckled, and Joshua joined in the laughter, easily able to picture Vivian acting so ornery.

Harrison added, "That lumpy thing she made was the saddest doll any of us'd ever seen. Pa ended up giving her the fancy doll on her birthday after all. I think he was impressed by her ingenuity."

As Joshua listened to her brothers' fond memories, more of his tension eased. Vivian was a smart, capable woman and, with Nate's help, they would survive. All three of them.

I'll bring you home, he silently promised her. *Just keep yourselves safe until I arrive.*

As they stood reminiscing while they watered their horses, the sound of running footsteps heading their way caught everyone's attention.

The men drew their weapons.

Gleason unsheathed a wickedly-sharp hunting knife from his boot.

And Joshua leveled his rifle toward the sound, cocked and ready.

Chapter 22

The tension had ridden higher than the sun, when Nate suddenly burst from between two large boulders to their left.

"Lower your weapons," Joshua yelled, shoving his rifle toward Gleason. He raced to his son, hauling the obviously battered and exhausted boy off his feet, into his arms, and embraced him tight. For a moment, Nate's small body collapsed against him and he hugged him back.

Then he pushed at Joshua's shoulders. "Put me down, we have to save her."

Joshua set him back on the ground, crouching down to eye level. Fury lodged in his chest. Morgan would pay for every bruise inflicted on this child. "Tell me."

Breathing heavy, Nate wiped tears from his dirt encrusted face. "We escaped, but Ma's real sick." His voice hitched. "She's been throwing up something awful."

Joshua's stomach dropped as he stood, glancing over at Harrison. "Must be the babe."

Not yet ready to lose physical contact with Nate, so great was his relief that the boy was safe, he kept one hand on his shoulder. But worry for his wife sat heavy in his heart.

"Where is she?" Harrison asked gently.

"We got away and hid in a cave, but she was too sick to go any further, so she sent me for help."

"Mount up," Joshua barked, slipping his boot into the stirrup and swinging into the saddle. He leaned down to grasp Nate's outstretched hand, lifting him up to rest in front of him so he could help support the exhausted boy. Joshua hadn't missed his son's chafed and bleeding wrists. One more reason Morgan had to pay. "How'd you escape?"

Nate sank back against him. "They tied us up in the mine, and when we heard them snoring, I broke free."

Ike spoke up. "How far'd you get before you found the cave?"

"Not sure. Took us maybe a couple hours, 'cause that woman hit Ma, and I know her head was hurting bad."

Joshua's hands tightened on the reins as an ice-cold rage filled every part of him. He'd never harmed a female before, but if any woman deserved punishment, it was Florence Johnson.

Frank's gritty, "Son of a bitch," mingled with Harrison's angry oath.

Joshua flicked his reins to get Quicksilver moving faster as worry for his wife and unborn child ate a hole in his gut.

~ ~ ~

So cold. So dark.

How long had she clung to the jagged stalagmite? Vivian wondered. It was the only thing keeping her from tumbling over the edge. Her arms numb, frozen into place, the smell of rotten eggs wafting off the mineral formation triggered an almost constant urge to throw up. After battling it back a half-dozen times, she lost the battle and hung her head as she vomited into the dark pit below her.

Finally, nearing collapse, she leaned against the fragile piece of rock saving her from certain death as tears filled her eyes.

Water dripping from the high ceiling soaked her bare shoulder where the sleeve seam had rent, falling one splotch at a time, until she thought madness might ensue. Her skirts had bunched up to the backs of her thighs on that terror-laden tumble from the passageway down to the place where the cavern yawned, wide and open. The pantalets beneath her clothing had torn, her tender skin stinging and abraded.

A sob escaped her throat when a small rock she'd dislodged from the stalagmite rolled away, bouncing off her arm. She never heard it land.

How far down had it dropped? Five feet? Fifty? In the smothering darkness it was impossible to know.

Shivering hard, she felt a sneeze coming on and held her breath until it passed. She couldn't sneeze, not now, not when her position was so precarious that moving a single wrong inch could send her to certain death.

If she had gone with Nate in search of Joshua.

If she had stayed near the opening of the cave instead of plunging blindly in.

If I'd never let my boy out of my sight in the first place.

"If, if," she chanted through chattering teeth.

A low, threatening growl answered.

The animalistic snarl frightened her worse than the realization Slim Morgan had come far too close to finding her. Something dangerous claimed this cave as a sanctuary. Coyote, mountain lion, even a bear, it didn't matter. Any of them would attack and maul.

Kill.

Her left leg cramped, a sudden, sharp pain. She'd pressed it tightly against the base of the stalagmite for stability, her other leg dangling over the edge. She bit back another sob as her calf spasmed.

I can't rub it out with my hand, I'd have to let go.

I can't let go, I'll slip.

I can't slip. I'll fall.

"Oh God, please. Please. Guide some help my way," she prayed on a breath of a whisper.

~ ~ ~

The gunshot came out of nowhere as they climbed higher. It pinged off a large boulder to Joshua's left.

"What the— Get down," he hissed. Dismounting fast, he yanked Nate from the saddle and shoved the reins in his hand. "Go with Mister Gleason." He met Gleason's bright blue gaze. The man nodded sharply, once.

Thankfully Nate didn't hesitate or protest. "Yessir." With the burly gambler hustling his son away and acting as a human shield, Joshua had one less worry.

Another bullet hit the ground a few feet away.

Frank crept up low, both Colts drawn. "Gotta be Morgan."

Spreading out along the trail, they took cover behind rocks and bushes. Ike climbed to a higher point, moving like a wraith on completely soundless feet. Joshua figured if they got out of this alive, he'd slap a deputy badge on the man and consider him hired.

"Morgan, you're surrounded."

A volley of shots sent Joshua and Harrison onto their bellies. Frank dropped to his knees, aimed both pistols, and let fly, shooting with deadly accuracy in the direction of the first shot.

A high-pitched, painful whinny rent the air. "Ah, Jesus," Frank snarled. "Not a horse."

Joshua shared his dismay at hurting an animal, though it meant a better chance of nabbing the bastard. "Morgan, there's no place to run."

"I got your woman, Lang." The taunting words sent a rancid mix of terror and fury through Joshua.

Frank released a string of curses that colored the air blue. "I'm going to cut off his balls and cram them down his throat."

Joshua wiped his sweaty face with his sleeve, thinking furiously. He had to put his trust in the knowledge that Vivian was resourceful and smart enough to keep herself from being found. Believing anything else would make him crazy. "If you've got my wife," he shouted, "prove it."

No answer. In the dead silence Joshua strained for any tiny speck of sound. Chancing a sideways glance toward the boulder where Gleason shielded Nate, he bit back a groan of relief when the man's massive frame hid Nate completely. The angle and size of the boulder worked in their favor, too. At least Nate was safe.

Joshua focused his attention back on the hillier area where the gunshots had come from. Deep down in his heart he knew Morgan was bluffing. He also knew the only way to be absolutely sure was to keep the bastard talking somehow as they eased up the trail and took him by surprise.

Lord, don't make me wrong here.

"Morgan, you listening?" Joshua shouted. "Show me my wife and I might not kill you dead."

~ ~ ~

The very first gunshot had scared Flo's aging nag. The skittish thing bolted, earning her a vicious slap to the face for not hitching the beast to a bush or scrub.

In the next flurry of bullets, Slim's horse screamed and went down as he and Flo ducked behind rocks. Crouching, she edged around a boulder and continued shooting, but found herself glancing over to where the animal lay on its side, its chest heaving, bleeding from its rear flank, high in the meaty area. She wouldn't put it past Slim to force the creature to carry him and then make her walk out.

In the echoing silence of spent gunshot, she'd begun reloading when a sharp neigh bleated. Flo turned as the wounded horse gained its feet, stumbling once. Tossing its mane, the animal galloped awkwardly away before she or Slim could react.

They were now stranded with no way out.

"Stupid slut." Slim backhanded her, catching the same cheek he'd hit before, the force of it pushing her against the rock. He yanked the gun from her loosened grip and shoved it into the waistband of his trousers.

Trying to catch her breath, fighting off a wave of pain, she fingered her cheek. The strong taste of blood coated her tongue as she eyed Slim warily, noting his wild expression. Suddenly she wanted nothing more than to get off the side of this ridge and away from Little Creede.

Away from Slim Morgan.

I'm still young enough to make a decent life for myself.

Saving her own bacon was the only important thing right now. Without a weapon her best bet was to sneak off around the rocks where she could better hide, then wait out the gunfire. Sooner or later Slim would run out of bullets.

As he grumbled and muttered, striding around in a circle and waving a pistol in the air, Flo crept away from her former lover, easing toward one of the back trails that led up and to the south of the Cascades. If she could get back to the cabin, she'd retrieve that little pouch of silver she knew Slim had hidden, months ago.

"Where the hell d'you think you're going?" His free hand came down heavy on her shoulder.

Throwing caution to the wind, Flo twisted and unbalanced him so he staggered on his bad leg. The shin bone had snapped from falling off Mineral Ridge all those months ago and had never healed right.

"I'm not staying around here to get shot at, you fool." Flo whirled and made to run but he caught a chunk of her hair and hauled her back. She landed on her knees with a pained grunt. "Let go!"

"You heard her, Morgan. Let her go. She'll face the judge for her crimes." The rough rasp came from the right, startling them both.

Slim yanked her to her feet and shoved her before him, as Joshua Lang continued, "I'd be more than happy to pump your ass full of lead, though. Where's my wife?"

An entire posse had snuck up on them while they fought. Flo bit back a frustrated hiss. Now she'd never get away.

The grip on her hair tightened until she thought he'd rip it right out of her head. "She's already dead." His cruel laughter rang in the air. "You think I'd leave her alive when I found her?"

Seeing an opening for some sort of escape, Flo shouted, "He didn't kill her."

"*Shut up.*" Slamming his hand around her throat, Slim cut off her air and squeezed until her eyes watered.

Choking, Flo felt the muzzle of his pistol at her temple. "No," she wheezed out. "Don't let him hurt me. I'll take you to your woman."

The hammer clicked so loudly in her ear, it sounded like a thunderclap.

Struggling to unpin her arms from Slim's crushing hold, she met the helpless fury in Joshua Lang's eyes as he advanced slowly, his attention focused tightly on them.

Then one of the Carter brothers—through her blurry vision she thought it might be Harrison—spoke up, his weapon trained on Slim at eye level. "Morgan, it's over. Make it easy on yourself and let Miss Johnson go."

The fact Harrison called her by a genteel name should have made her feel rotten for all the bad things she'd done in her life. Whoring herself out, arson, assault . . . aiding and abetting a convicted murderer. But one thing Flo prided herself on not being was a hypocrite. She'd lived the life she chose and wouldn't apologize for any of it.

That didn't mean she couldn't take her treacherous former lover down with her.

Sagging in his arms, she managed a gulp of fortifying air. "I've got enough on Morgan to hang him," she gasped harshly. Before anyone could react, she whipped up one hand and dug her nails into his face, aiming for any kind of distraction.

Slim howled, jerking away. "You ignorant, worthless whore."

For a single moment she saw the sheriff and his men rush them, saw guns raised and heard hammers cocked. Her lips curved in the first real smile she'd felt in ages.

Bang, bang, you're dead, you bastard.

The last thing Flo heard was the shouts of the men surrounding them.

The last thing she felt was the hot, agonizing burn.

~ ~ ~

In the fury of gunfire that followed, Joshua's only satisfaction came from seeing Slim Morgan's body jumping as bullets riddled him from all sides.

Won't be walking away this time.

As the dust settled, he dropped his shooting arm, his hand aching from gripping the Colt too hard, his breathing choppy. From the corner of his eye he spotted Ike slithering down from a higher perch and nodded at the sharpshooter. He'd no doubt that first bullet—the one hitting dead center of Morgan's forehead—came from Ike's gun.

Frank stepped to his side, his face grimy with dirt and sweat. "I wanted the woman to face prison time, not to get killed." He stared at the dead couple, Florence Johnson still pinned against Morgan in a bloody embrace.

"Yeah." Joshua wiped his face with the bandana tied loosely around his neck. He studied the bodies sprawled on the ground. Florence Johnson didn't look so pretty anymore with half her head blown off by Morgan, right before Joshua's posse filled the bastard full of lead.

"Pa!" The young, scared voice whipped him around, and

Joshua dropped to one knee as Nate tore up the rough trail toward him.

He gathered the boy close, a hand going to his head to hold his face against his shoulder and block the sight of Morgan and the woman. Despite everything they'd put this child through, they were still his folks, and Joshua wasn't sure how Nate would react, how he'd get past what had been done to him. And now, to them. It was an awful thing to have to live with regardless of the circumstances.

"Let me see." Nate squirmed in his arms.

Joshua tightened his grasp. "No, son. You don't want to see this."

Nate eased back and set his palm against Joshua's cheek, his gaze weary, but steady. "Please, Pa. I need to see."

With a rough sigh, Joshua slackened his arms, allowing Nate to scramble away. Rising to his feet, hating to think of Nate facing this kind of violence but understanding the necessity, Joshua watched him approach the bodies.

For long seconds, Nate stared down at what remained of Slim Morgan and Florence Johnson. Joshua couldn't imagine what went through his mind, only the tight line of his body giving away any emotion.

"Nate," Joshua began, wanting to get him away from the death and the blood.

But the boy shook his head, venturing closer, until he stood directly over Slim's inert form. Nate's throat worked, and Joshua came forward, primed to deal with some kind of outburst.

Nate bent and spat on the man who had given him life, then tried to take away everything a boy held most dear.

Joshua blinked at the unexpected reaction, while next to him Frank muttered, "Will you look at that."

Nate straightened and turned to face them. "Can we go get my ma, now?"

Chapter 23

Nate leaned forward in the saddle and pointed toward a higher cluster of caves. "There."

Joshua squinted in the morning sun, studying the area Nate indicated. "Which one?"

"Middle. It looked safer." Nate peered over his shoulder and met Joshua's gaze, appearing as weary and desperate as Joshua felt. "She promised she wouldn't go anywhere. She promised she'd wait right where I left her." His voice shook. "She wouldn't leave, would she?"

Joshua hastened to assure the boy, tightening his arm around Nate's waist as Quicksilver picked his way carefully over and between rocks and sharp-edged stones. "No, son. When your ma makes a promise, she keeps it." He glanced over at Frank, riding to his left, Harrison a bit beyond, followed closely by Gleason and Ike. "We should walk in from here. Too many rocks for the horses to maneuver."

"Agreed." Harrison swung down and draped Copper's reins over a spindly scrub bush, while the other three men followed suit.

Handing Nate down into Frank's waiting arms, Joshua jumped to the ground and tied Quicksilver to a withered hackberry stump. He tightened the leg ties on his holster while Harrison looped a water canteen over his shoulder. "Let's go."

Nate sidled close and Joshua brought him in for a fast hug. "Lead the way, partner."

With Nate ahead of him, Joshua kept one eye on his boy and the other on the surrounding area. Unease slid through him. Animals often made dens in secluded caves high in the mountains. "Nate, did you notice if the cave was clear of animal dung?"

Nate paused as Joshua came abreast. "It was still dark when we went in." His young face creased with fresh worry before he broke into a clumsy run. "We gotta hurry."

Joshua caught up easily and grabbed his arm. "Slow down. There's no trail here." As Nate sucked in a few uneven breaths, Joshua pushed the sweat-soaked hair from the boy's forehead, staring ahead to the caves. This high up, he knew these natural sanctuaries looked deceptively safe from the front, when they were anything but.

Frank came abreast, Harrison following close behind. "What's wrong?" the elder Carter demanded.

"Maybe nothing." Joshua pointed toward the rock where discoloration had set in layers of reddish rock. "I've noticed that in cavern areas. I don't like seeing it here." He waited for Ike and Gleason to reach them. "Either of you got matchsticks? We might need them."

Gleason nodded shortly. "Ah've got some." He patted a pocket in his trousers. "Let's go git yer lil' gal, Sheriff."

They approached the opening quietly, Nate pulling against Joshua's hand, eager to run in. Mindful of the dangers and concerned about the cougar scat he'd spotted on the ground to the side of the entrance, Joshua held the boy firmly. "Easy now."

Inside the cave a sour odor lingered, mixed with the stink of sulphur. "She got sick a few times," Nate confided. "I didn't want to leave her." He pointed toward a rock wall. "We went over there. Slept a little, too."

"Vivian?" Joshua called softly, moving toward a curve in the rock wall. If she still slept, he was loath to wake her, but they needed to get away from here before the cave's regular occupants returned. Venturing closer, his heart plummeted to see dusty smears on the ground where she and Nate must have lain.

She wasn't there.

Panic swamped him, unlike any he'd ever experienced. "Vivian!" His shout echoed oddly.

Frank grabbed his shoulder as Harrison stepped up behind Nate and caught him before he could go running. "I'd bet this opens up into a cavern," Frank murmured. "Look over there." He indicated the beginning of a passageway. "Think she could have gone that way?"

"Hope not." Cavern passages were tricky enough, the way they could snake around high and low spots. It was how they often ended that was most dangerous. "If she took the passage God only knows where she might land. It'd be blacker than the gates of Hell in there."

Ike spoke up. "I've got a long hank of rope." He peered into the darkness beyond. "It'll come in handy. Awful dim in there. Might grab some pork grease, too." He shrugged at the odd looks Harrison and Frank shot him. "I bring it along when I take Levi on the range with me. Use it for all kinds of things."

"Go get both." Joshua figured if they needed a torch of some kind, grease would keep it burning as well as anything.

Silently Gleason doled out matchsticks while they waited for Ike to return. With everyone in place and Nate close on his heels, Joshua advanced into the passageway, his boots thudding on the stone. Trailing one hand against the wall, he felt carefully, able to see less and less the further he walked. "It's tight in here," he called to the men bringing up the rear. "You might have to crawl."

A grunt of acknowledgement responded, and Joshua pushed ahead.

Suddenly the ground dipped alarmingly. "Ah, shit." Joshua fumbled for a matchstick and scraped it on the rocks until it flared. Holding it out, all the blood left his head as he spotted the way the stone floor sloped into inky nothingness. "Vivian!"

"Help . . ." The voice echoed, weak and shaky, yet it was the sweetest sound Joshua'd ever heard.

"Vivian!" Tossing caution aside, he ordered tersely, "Stay put, Nate," before rushing forward, uncaring of the danger. Heart pounding in his ears, Joshua hastily lit another matchstick, the slight flare flickering as it burned fast.

He held the flame higher.

And groaned, his knees nearly buckling under him at the sight of his wife, clinging precariously to a chunk of limestone, at least thirty feet down a slippery-looking incline.

Behind him, Frank hissed, "Jesus have mercy."

In the second before the matchstick burnt out, she raised a tearstained face, eyes glassy. "Joshua . . .?"

~ ~ ~

I must be dreaming.

Blinking dust and grit from her eyes, Vivian fought to focus in the sudden glow. Was that really Joshua standing above? Her brothers, too?

"Vivian, don't move," Joshua shouted. "Shit! Someone bring me that rope."

More voices joined his, too muffled to understand exactly what they were saying, but she recognized Nate's voice. Her relief at knowing he was safe quelled some of her fear.

"It's going to be all right, angel," Joshua called to her. "We're going to get you up from there."

Before she could ask how on earth they were going to accomplish that, a torch lit the area from above just as a small figure slid down the treacherous slope toward where she hung on for dear life.

"Nate, no," she croaked. Beyond the relief at knowing she'd been found, pure terror gripped her as the child she and

Joshua had claimed inched his way along the stone ground on his belly. A rope coiled around his chest, and more rope hung crossways on his shoulder. "Go back!"

"Pa and Uncle Frank's got me." Nate's young voice suddenly sounded a whole lot more grown-up. "I told 'em I needed to come rescue you."

"Oh, Nate." She lowered her head and wept. "Please go back," she pleaded. "It's too dangerous." In her mind she saw him roll, drop over the edge, and fall, a nightmare vision that wouldn't go away. "Don't come any closer."

"Angel, do as Nate says." Joshua's demand echoed in the huge open space. "We've got him firm, and we're gonna pull you both up."

Helplessly Vivian watched, heart in her throat, as Nate advanced a foot at a time, his grimy little face tight and his lower lip caught between his teeth in concentration. Closer and closer he slid, his father and uncle feeding out the rope slowly, until he stretched one hand to touch her arm.

Every muscle in her body ached to gather him up and hold him, but she couldn't let go of the stalagmite for even a second.

Nate edged nearer and laid his head against her shoulder, careful not to jostle her. The feel of his cheek set off fresh tears that clogged Vivian's throat until she could barely breathe.

"Hi, Ma," he said calmly. "Ready to go?"

~ ~ ~

Someday I'll think of this with pride. But not today. The sight of Nate slithering down a slope toward the edge of the world made Joshua dizzy from worry instead. Overwhelming guilt too, because he'd allowed the boy to persuade him.

Please, Pa, he'd begged, let me go. I can do it.

Nate was thin but surprisingly strong, agile as a monkey. He'd be the easiest for them to pull back up to safety with

Vivian's weight, though slight, added to the rope. Still, Joshua experienced the kind of panic that could send a man into insanity as the life-or-death drama unfolded before their eyes, all of them helpless to do anything other than steady the rope.

And pray.

Gleason held the makeshift torch high, his exceptional height a godsend. Harrison had donated his shirt, torn up, wadded around a scrub limb, and streaked with pork grease. Next to him, Ike stood with his own shirt in hand, prepared to set it alight once the first torch burned out. It wouldn't last forever, and Joshua swallowed back fear that they'd run out of limb and light before Nate could secure the rope around Vivian.

She couldn't let go of the limestone to raise her arms long enough for Nate to slip the noose around her. While they waited above, Nate finally resorted to sliding the untied end from back to front, bringing it through the actual noose loop and securing it snug at her waist.

"Nate," Joshua instructed, hoping his tone conveyed confidence, "pull the end through your rope and make a square knot like I showed you."

Silently, Nate worked the rough hemp with a steady hand, forming a knot that looked as if it would hold. In just a few minutes Nate had tied Vivian's rope to the one securing him and knotted the excess so they could hold on to each other.

"Good job, son." Joshua's voice roughened with emotion. "Now, keep your mother close, and don't look down. Vivian," he urged, "let go of the rock and we'll pull you up."

"I can't move." Vivian sent him a despairing look. "I can't lift my arms."

"Angel, just let go."

"Ma, I can help." Nate placed his hands on her shoulders and rubbed carefully. "You won't fall 'cause you're tied to me and Pa's got the other end."

Softly, he continued to murmur to her, reassurances or encouragement—or both—Joshua had no idea. But it worked, because her shoulders, then her arms, relaxed, and she leaned back against Nate. As soon as she did, he wrapped himself around her like vines. "We're ready."

"Easy does it, men," Frank muttered, bracing himself behind Joshua. "Harrison?"

"Ready when you are. Gleason's got the end."

"Ah tied it to mah leg. Ain't goin' nowhere. Yew jest tell me when," Gleason boomed out.

"Ike?"

Light flared. "Got a fresh torch." Ike raised it high. "It'll last a while."

"All right, then." Joshua sent up a string of prayers and tightened his grip on the rope, his eyes never leaving his precious wife and son.

"*Pull.*"

~ ~ ~

The trip back to town was only bearable because Vivian clung to her husband and was able to keep Nate in view as he nodded sleepily against his uncle's broad shoulder. Harrison held him so gently, easing his horse along, the stallion seeming to understand he carried a priceless burden.

Never had she been so terrified than to see Nate, dangling on the end of a rope, sliding down to her with such calm assurance on his face. He'd had to be scared out of his mind, yet his hands never trembled as he'd expertly fastened the rope around her.

Somehow they'd made it safely up the stone slope, clinging together while Joshua and the rest of the men reeled in the rope. Now, snuggling closer to Joshua, she let her mind drift, for the first time in days allowing herself to fully relax.

She ached from head to toe—*every single toe*—and the backs of her legs felt raw. Wrapped in not only Joshua's shirt but Mister Gleason's waistcoat as well, she finally felt warm, though she swam in the flamboyant gambler's expensive, brocaded garment. Still, when he'd offered it so gallantly, she'd never have refused.

"We're almost to the turnoff for the edge of town." Joshua's lips traced over the lump on her forehead, one of many lumps and bruises on her body. "Are you all right to go on or do you need to rest?"

She hastened to assure him, lifting her cheek from his shoulder and turning a bit to meet his anxious regard. "I can make it. I'm sore but so much better. The gallon of water you forced me to drink might have helped." As a teasing remark it wasn't much, but it made her husband smile. "We won't discuss that hardtack I about broke my teeth on, though it did have a tasty coating."

He snorted. "That was Ike Barnes' contribution to your recovery. He puts pork grease on everything."

"Oh, my." *Feels good to laugh instead of cry.* For several minutes they were silent, plodding along slowly in the afternoon sun.

Joshua had already answered some of Vivian's questions regarding the final minutes of Slim Morgan and Florence Johnson's lives. She sensed he'd glossed over the worst which concerned her menfolk's participation, things she needed to know. "Nate hasn't said much about Morgan. Or the woman." She would never refer to Florence by her full name again. "Please tell me Nate didn't see them die."

When Joshua didn't answer right away, Vivian moaned, "Joshua, no."

He expelled a harsh breath but drew her closer. "Rest your head, angel." Obligingly Vivian relaxed against his shoulder and sighed when he brought his lips to her ear. "Someday you might want to ask Nate yourself and I'm sure he'll want to talk about it. But for now, I'll tell you that young'un showed amazing bravery even before we went in the cave after you. He faced his enemies with fortitude and courage."

For Vivian, in that moment, it was enough.

As the outskirts of town came into view, Knight Gleason cantered closer, his powerful stallion snorting and tossing his magnificent mane. "Ma'am." He tipped the rim of his fancy Stetson. "Ah'm fixin' to head to mah gamblin' establishment an' see what trouble mah staff has got theyselves into."

"Mister Gleason, I don't know how to thank you for your help and your kindness." Vivian held out a hand as Joshua reined in, Gleason following suit. Fisting the reins in one large paw, he carefully took her hand and gave it a gentle squeeze. Ignoring his stallion's sideways dance, he leaned over far enough to bring her knuckles to his lips for a courtly kiss.

"It was mah honor to serve, Missus Lang." He released her hand with a wink, shot a salute to Joshua, then gave his mount free rein, the stallion tearing down the widening trail.

"I'll bet Miss Hannah will be glad to see him," Vivian mused. "Not to mention his poor niece."

Joshua urged his own stallion to catch up to Harrison and Frank. "I'm sure of it, as well as everyone else in town all waiting anxiously for you and Nate." Joshua came abreast of Harrison's burnished mustang.

Ike Barnes had already split off toward home, the small farm he and his son, Levi, tended a few miles out of town. Volunteering to deal with the bodies left behind on the side of the ridge, Ike would bring his wagon up the trail tomorrow.

Nate's head popped up from Harrison's shoulder. He waved at her. "I fell asleep."

"Snoring, too," Harrison teased, his free hand ruffling the boy's hair.

Vivian grinned, then a cheer snagged her attention and she gaped as Joshua, Harrison, and Frank guided the horses toward Main Street. The usually quiet boardwalk teemed with people. "What on earth—?"

Joshua halted next to the nearest hitching post. "Welcome home, angel."

When Vivian spotted her mother and Dub hurrying toward them, her eyes blurred with tears. "Mama."

Dub reached her first and held up his hands as Joshua loosened his arms around her. "Get down here, daughter." He swung Vivian off the horse's broad back and set her on her feet with a hard, rocking hug, rumbling out a chuckle as her mother caught her next in a perfumed embrace. Vivian clung as Mama alternately laughed and cried, kissed and fretted as only a mother could do.

Surrounded by family and friends, passed from one set of arms to another and kissed to within an inch of her very life, Vivian soaked up the love of an entire town, feeling very lucky as she met Joshua's tender regard. He moved to her side and slipped an arm around her shoulders as Nate ran over and huddled against her bedraggled, dusty clothing.

"Doc's gonna want to see you as soon as we can break away from this madhouse," he murmured.

Too happy to balk at being examined in such an intimate way, Vivian merely replied, "All right."

Later, she'd settle in and answer some of the questions shouted her way. But for now, standing in the circle of her husband's embrace and holding tight to their son, Vivian wanted for nothing else.

Chapter 24

Resplendent in burgundy from head to toe, Knight Gleason bent his bride over one arm and dipped her low, planting a kiss on her lips that must have curled Hannah's toes inside her pretty satin slippers.

Amid applause and whoops echoing off the church rafters, Vivian poked Joshua in the side when he wolf-whistled the loudest. "Stop that. This is a dignified affair." Meeting her husband's amused gaze, she burst into laughter at the way his eyebrows waggled. "Well, maybe not so dignified."

Joshua grunted. "The groom is no milquetoast. Neither is Hannah, I'm wagering."

They both watched the brand-new Mister and Missus Gleason meander down the aisle to the antechamber. Hannah's lace-trimmed gauze veil now sat a bit crookedly on the top of her head and a lock of pale brown hair had escaped the snug chignon Catherine had fashioned an hour earlier, but her face glowed, her cheeks rosy and her eyes bright with happiness. Knight swept her along carefully, matching his long stride to her smaller, daintier steps. Beneath his bushy red beard and thick moustache, the man's grin almost split his face in two.

Rising, Joshua held out his arm. "Shall we go offer our best wishes to the bride and groom?"

Vivian stood and shook out the folds of her favorite lavender gown. "Certainly, Sheriff."

They joined the noisy queue waiting to shake hands, clap the groom's back, and hug the bride. Most of the town had shown up for the wedding, with everyone invited for a reception of cake and champagne at the Stage House. Vivian and Joshua drew closer to the receiving line, easing in behind Retta, Harrison, and the children.

Magnolia Sanders stood next to her uncle, stunning in a peach-toned, silk and taffeta confection that could only have come from a high-end shop back East. Offering a smile, she held out a hand as delicate and pale as the flower she'd been named for. "Missus Lang," she murmured, her voice charmingly musical.

Vivian clasped the young woman's fingers. "Delighted to see you here, Miss Magnolia. That's a lovely gown."

"Please, call me Maggie." She spread her slightly gathered skirts and held them out. "I thought it a bit much for a wedding, for I would never want to outshine my new auntie, bless her sweet lil' heart." Magnolia—*Maggie*—leaned in. "I'm so happy Uncle Knight found someone to love."

"We are, too." Impulsively, Vivian drew her in for a hug. "I hope to visit with you at length, before you head back East."

Drawing back, Maggie formed a blinding smile. "Count on it."

Closing in on the happy couple, Vivian caught the wink Knight shot over his bride's head, and winked back. The big, brash Georgia gambler had fast become one of her favorite people.

She reached Hannah's side, and found herself gathered into a tight embrace. "You look so very lovely, Missus Gleason," Vivian whispered in her ear.

Hannah drew back, clasping Vivian's hands. "I'm floating on a cloud. And I feel like a princess." Created from ivory beaded satin, Hannah's wedding gown boasted a softly gathered bodice draped low over her upper arms, caught up in delicate rosettes. A wide sash emphasized her tiny waist, and the bell-shaped skirts swept the floor into a train embellished with more rosettes. She did indeed look like a princess.

Leaning in, Vivian brushed a kiss on Hannah's cheek. "May your life ahead with your handsome husband echo with love and many giggling children."

"Oh, my. I do so hope for children." Hannah's soft brown gaze lowered to Vivian's waist, where the seams of her gown had been let out. "When are you due, my dear?"

Now Vivian flushed as she placed a hand over her mostly flat tummy. "Doc says about seven months from now."

They shared a moment of womanly camaraderie, before Vivian moved aside to shake Knight's hand.

He beamed down at her, then swept her into a hug that stole her breath. "Yew and yer auntie have mah everlastin' gratitude fer helpin' mah lil' lady prepare for the weddin'." He set Vivian back on her feet carefully, then his eyes strayed to his blushing bride. The adoration there made Vivian's throat tighten with emotion.

"Ah sweah, when ah saw her walkin' down the aisle to me, ah thought ah'd died an' gone to the pearly gates." He released a gusty sigh. "Nevah seen anythin' so angel-like in mah life."

"Your bride is beautiful, inside and out, Mister Gleason," Vivian murmured. "I'm thrilled for you both, that you found each other."

"Yes, ma'am. Ah'm a lucky man."

~ ~ ~

Standing near the bar in the Stage House's main salon, Joshua smiled down at the ravishing woman currently holding his hand as she tapped her toe in time to Dub's spirited fiddling.

"I ask the man to play a waltz so I can dance with my wife, and he plays two reels in a row," Joshua mock-grumbled, earning him a pinch in the side.

"Hush. Mister Gleason *is* Irish, after all. For that matter, so is Dub, on his mother's side. Though I'll wager we'll get at least one round of "Beautiful Dreamer" out of him before the reception's over." She leaned her head on his coat sleeve, pointing toward the edge of the dance floor where Robert Blackwood hovered, a glass partway to his lips, staring across the room as if poleaxed. "Your young deputy just discovered an Irish rose."

"Huh?" Joshua looked in the direction of her finger, seeing the new Missus Gleason chatting with the very pretty Magnolia. "She does have uncommonly bright hair," he noted.

"Not the hair, silly man. Take a gander at the look on Robert's face." Vivian caught hold of Joshua's jaw and turned him until he could see his deputy as well as his expression.

The man *did* appear to have been knocked sideways. Joshua released a soft chuckle. "He's in way over his head with that one. She's got finishing school written all over her."

Indeed, the besotted Robert had strode the length of the room and now stood before Magnolia, his lips moving while he held out his arm. As Joshua and Vivian watched, the young woman blushed furiously, but took his hand and let him swing her into what was left of the reel. Robert's face reflected stunned joy as he led her around with more enthusiasm than skill.

"Hope her feet survive the stomping they're sure to get," Joshua said. "Her daddy might have to buy her a new pair of shoes."

"I heard the man is a lawyer, so I'm sure he can afford it." Vivian moved to stand in front of him, her hand outstretched in much the same pose as Robert's. Mischief shone in her amber eyes. "May I have this dance?"

"Little minx, that's *my* line." Joshua gathered her into his arms as Dub plied his bow in the opening notes of the promised waltz.

Circling the polished wide-planked floor with his angel, Joshua leaned down and whispered into her ear. "You like taking the lead, Missus Sheriff Lang?"

A delicious shiver was his only answer, as she peered up at him with a widening smile, pressing her body closer.

Epilogue

Unpinning her wide-brimmed straw boater, Vivian set the ribbon-bedecked confection on her dresser. The ride back to the ranch had been a breezy one in the open carriage, the late-autumn weather nippy. Her woolen shawl, combined with the heat of Joshua's body as he'd encouraged her to lean back against him, had kept her warm enough.

Drifting to the window, Vivian gazed out at the expanse of yard and beyond, a lower valley where Bonney Creek wound along the Carter property line. While she loved it here, the idea of building a home in Little Creede, just for her, Joshua, and Nate—and the tiny one nestled safely in her womb—thrilled her.

A plot of land past the edge of town had already been set aside for the new school. Joshua had secured adjoining acreage for their own house. Breaking ground on both would begin in the spring. In the meantime, the cozy ranch house would keep them warm through the winter months.

She caressed her stomach, anticipating the day she held her babe in her arms, Joshua cradling them both in his strong embrace as they looked out over the town which had already given them so much.

With a smile, Vivian closed the curtains against the encroaching twilight.

Mama and Dub had sent everyone home, declaring they would help Catherine clean up after the reception, so Retta and Harrison shared their carriage with Vivian and Joshua. Sitting in the back with a twin in each arm, Vivian had teased and tickled her nephews, eliciting giggles, while Addie taught Jenny the words to "Beautiful Dreamer."

From the porch of their ranch she and Joshua had stood and waved as Harrison and Retta headed for home with their rowdy brood.

Now, pleasantly tired, her usual nausea at bay for a change, Vivian smoothed her hand over her upswept hair as she opened her lingerie drawer, pausing when she touched soft linen and the worn edge of old leather.

The book.

Her curiosity and fascination with the hand-painted drawings had not lessened a bit. Nor had her frustration with the way her husband treated her like a delicate china doll that couldn't be touched, only seen and admired.

Three weeks had passed since her and Nate's rescue on Lower Cascade Mountain. Doc Sheaton had, in his blunt, forthright manner, explained she and Joshua could resume their marital relations. Joshua hadn't said a word, only nodded, but the look he'd leveled at her had made her heat up from head to toe. Longing, desire, need, it was all there in his intense, hazel eyes.

And yet, he hadn't touched her. Not how she longed to be touched.

Oh, at first she'd loved the way he'd hovered over her with such tenderness and caring. She'd soaked it up as greedily as water disappeared into a sponge that'd been left out in the sun too long. But all her aches and pains were gone now, and she needed more from him.

While Joshua doled out hay and oats to the horses, Vivian flipped through the book. Her heart raced, imagining his hands on her in the same manner as some of the drawings on the pages. For once, she wanted him to let go of that tight control he kept over himself the few times he'd made love to her. She wasn't fragile or weak, and though the stubborn man hadn't said the words, she knew his heart. And her heart told her Joshua loved her, even if he didn't realize it yet.

Sudden nervousness assailed her but she wasn't about to back down. During the Gleasons' reception, a plan had formed. Arranging for Nate to stay with Retta overnight had been easy, for Nate loved his new cousins.

I'm going to take the lead, Joshua, and seduce you.

Proud of her own daringness, Vivian hoped she had the courage to go through with it, since she wasn't exactly sure what to do.

Studying a few of the drawings, she decided she needed less apparel. She wasn't brave enough to approach Joshua naked. Still, the pretty nightdress Catherine had loaned her for the occasion should work. Huddled in a side salon at the Stage House after the wedding cake had been served, she'd discussed her plans with Retta and Catherine. A smart move, for they'd given her some pointers.

Then Catherine had subtly taken the back stairs to her private suite, returning with a soft bundle folded into a drawstring bag.

Vivian hurried over to place the book on the table nestled against Joshua's side of the bed, before crossing to the dresser to retrieve the nightdress. Thanking the heavens above for the front-fastening increasing corset Retta had given her, she got out of her clothing easily and, naked, lifted the sheer material over her head. It floated around her like a gossamer cloud, before settling over her curves in the most scandalous way.

She liked it. Vivian removed a handful of hairpins, then picked up her boar bristle brush.

A few minutes later the sound of her husband, slamming the kitchen door, brought a smile to her lips. Ignoring the jumpy butterflies in her tummy that she couldn't quite contain, she called out, "In here."

His footsteps moved toward the bedroom, and she could hardly breathe, so caught up in the anticipation of his reaction. She'd brushed her long hair until it lay like silk down her back and dabbed some rosewater behind her ears.

She pinched her cheeks and gently bit her lips to add some color. Her anticipation grew, her nipples peaking against the sheer material of her gown, as he trudged down the short hallway.

Joshua strode inside, stumbling to a halt when he spotted her. His eyes darkened before his gaze slowly lowered over her and back up, pausing at her breasts, before finally locking gazes with her. The hunger, so plain to see on his face, helped settle her, and her tense muscles relaxed, even as desire washed through her.

"Angel," he murmured in a husky whisper.

"Joshua," she teased back, happiness bubbling up inside her. He wanted her as badly as she wanted him. Determined to get past his reserves, tonight she'd make him see her for what she was, a strong woman ready to live a full and wondrous life with him.

"What are you doing?" He took a step toward her.

"Waiting for you." She met his advance with one of her own.

His Adam's apple jerked as he swallowed, his expression tightening. "You need time to recover." Yet, as if drawn by an invisible force, he edged closer.

She smiled and matched his stride, their gazes locked on each other, until there was only one small bit of space separating them.

"Doc Sheaton said everything is fine. I'm fine. The baby is fine." Unwilling to wait another second to be in his arms, Vivian closed the final distance between them, slipping her arms around his neck. "So please be quiet and kiss me."

He stared into her eyes for a long moment, bringing up a hand to brush across the fading bruise on her cheek. "I'm sorry you were hurt. When I think of how close I came to losing . . ."

"Shh," she murmured, standing on tiptoe to press her mouth to his, cutting off his words, twining her fingers through the thick silky hair loose on his shoulders.

His hands grasped her hips as she crowded closer, until she could feel the tension in every line of his body. Breaking the kiss, he murmured, "You need more time." Instead of pushing her away as she thought he might, he held her tighter, the evidence of his desire hard against her stomach.

The man thought far too much. Worried far too much. Her husband was a strong, kind, honorable man who showed his love to her every day.

Vivian adored him, would continue to tell him so until he was ready to return the words. But she didn't need them. Deep inside she knew.

Joshua loved her.

Loved Nate.

Loved this baby she carried.

That was enough. That was everything.

She flicked her tongue against his lips. Once. Twice. Three times, before he growled, delving into her mouth the same way she wanted him in her body. Moving to the bed, he brought her down onto the mattress, his muscled frame sprawling across her as he continued to kiss her like he never wanted to stop.

Vivian writhed beneath him as his kisses went on for an eternity, one of his hands gently cradling her head, the other caressing her body.

When he suddenly lifted away, she moaned in protest, only to have him slide the fragile satin ribbons of her nightdress down her arms, baring her to the waist. The clamp of his mouth around her nipple made her arch her back as the pleasure from his greedy suction shot straight to her core.

Without letting go, he tugged the delicate material the rest of the way down and flung it over his shoulder.

She cried out his name as his hand slid to the juncture of her thighs and he thrummed her pearl, sending tiny shockwaves of bliss through her.

She needed more.

"Joshua," she pleaded, widening her legs.

He brought his face a scant inch from hers, his eyes dark and intent as two fingers breached her sensitive opening, pressing deep. "What do you want, Wife?" he asked, as he began a sensual dance inside her, sending toe-curling trembles through her.

"That," she murmured, her eyes slamming shut as she lifted her hips to his touch, "more of that." Her demand became a rapturous sob as he flicked her pearl again and sent her flying.

~ ~ ~

Joshua's heart pounded, watching Vivian find her pleasure. She was so lovely, the most beautiful woman he'd ever seen. He'd be forever grateful she belonged to him. And she loved him, though he didn't deserve her. Lord knew he loved her beyond reason, and he planned to spend the rest of his days proving to her she'd made the right choice to be his wife.

Maybe it's time you told her that, jackass.

She collapsed back onto the mattress. Eyes closed, her breasts, already appearing fuller, rose and fell enticingly as she regained her breath.

He placed his hand on her belly, where his child lay within. *Past time.*

Her eyelids slowly lifted, satisfaction in the look she shared with him. Stretching her hands over her head, she purred, and Joshua's body throbbed at the breathtaking sight.

Forever mine . . .

His hand stroking her from hip to breast, he leaned in to nibble her kiss-reddened lips. "I love you, angel, with everything in me."

Her eyes softened, and if love had a look, that was definitely it.

The hole in Joshua's chest he'd lived with, most of his life, now overflowed with love for the sweetest, most beautiful woman who'd ever walked God's green earth.

Vivian brought her hand up to cup one side of his face. "I know. I love you, too."

His cock, painfully hard beneath the buttons of his trousers, jumped at her words. How he needed to lose himself inside the tight clasp of her body. But she wasn't ready. Holding her was enough for tonight. They'd have the rest of their lives together. Ignoring the ache in his balls, he rolled to the side, tugging her close. "I've loved you for a long time and I should have told you sooner."

She stared at him with such tenderness, Joshua felt about ten feet tall. "It doesn't matter, we're together now."

Then to his surprise, she reached for his suspenders, tugging on the front fasteners. By the time his brain engaged, she huffed in exasperation. "Lift up, Joshua."

Amusement and lust boiled inside him as he did as she requested. "What are you doing?"

"What do you think I'm doing?" Plucking at the last fastener, Vivian tossed the suspenders aside. Rising to her knees, her breasts bouncing mere inches from his face, making his mouth water for another taste, she started on his shirt buttons. He eagerly helped her strip off his clothes, until she'd straddled him, her damp womanly flesh a temptation against his stomach.

Somehow he managed to keep his hands to himself, curious to see what she was up to. This wasn't a position he'd have thought Vivian knew.

Joshua set his arms flat on the mattress on either side of him, not about to intrude on her play. Though he read some hesitation in her eyes and noted the blush rising to her cheeks, he was determined to let her lead.

"I want—" She nibbled her bottom lip. "I want to try something."

Unsure of what to expect but admittedly more curious than ever, Joshua brought one hand to her hip and stroked gently. "I'm all yours, Missus Lang."

She leaned in and kissed his mouth lingeringly, then eased away. "I might require some . . . assistance." Her voice held a slight unsteadiness.

He bit back a chuckle, reluctant to make her uncomfortable yet dying to know what sort of magic she might have planned. "Whatever you need."

If he had to lash himself to the bed to hold back his urge to control their lovemaking, he would. When she bestowed a final kiss to his lips and swung around until she sat on his chest, facing the other way, Joshua's jaw dropped.

"Goddamn," he groaned, both hands going to her hips in a stabilizing gesture as she rose to her knees. Mink brown tendrils tumbling down the elegant curve of her back, her shapely buttocks wriggling into position, she took what little breath he had left in his lungs clean away.

She looked over her shoulder at him, wide-eyed as she attempted to adjust herself. "Joshua, I can't quite . . . help, please?"

"Just relax." He placed one large hand against the small of her back as his other palmed his cock. Easing her forward, he maneuvered their bodies until she could take him in.

Every ounce of restraint he thought he could drum up paled at the feel of her enveloping him. Her first hesitant movements were awkward, but before long she caught the rhythm of their lovemaking, and the glide of her body had him clenching his teeth against the pleasure.

So seductive and sensual, he could barely hang on to the tattered edges of his own control. Yet his heart filled with joy.

My precious wife.

Then all thought fled, save the need to help her find her release and share it with her. As she moaned and rode him faster, Joshua sat up until he could better reach her breasts. Cupping them, he supported her easily, the feel of her tight nipples against his palms pure torture. A keening cry escaped her as she leaned against his chest, and knowing he wouldn't last much longer, he slid one hand to her nub and flicked the tender flesh, sending her body into spasms, as her tight channel clamped around him like a vise.

His own release overtook him, his only thought a deep thankfulness for this woman who was made for him, and only him.

~ ~ ~

Sated pleasure still coursed through her as she collapsed back on her husband. Vivian sighed blissfully. "That was fun."

Joshua grunted. "I think you killed me." Lifting her by the hips, he eased her away, then turned her until she could prop herself on his chest as he sprawled across the bed.

Smiling down at him, the residual shivers from his body delighted her. "I hope to kill you a few more times tonight, Husband."

The love in his eyes made her world perfect. One brow quirked. "Where did you learn that?"

Reaching past him, Vivian lifted her now-favorite book off the table and held it up in front of his face. "Like any good student, I have study material."

Joshua's mouth dropped open as he gaped at the revealing drawing on the cover, framed in worn-out leather binding. "I— Holy—" The snort he released grew into a chuckle that became a full-bodied belly laugh, until Vivian joined in to the point of tears.

His laughter abruptly stopped, and he rolled her underneath him. He stared down at her, the humor in his eyes replaced by pure hunger.

For her. Joshua accepted her as more than his innocent wife. Now he saw her as a woman. A woman he desired. Loved.

Needed.

He knuckled a strand of hair from her cheek. "What adventures we'll share. Just wait and see."

Happier than she'd ever been in her life, Vivian nodded, imagining a lifetime with this man. Joshua hefted her book, opening it to a most intriguing drawing. She glanced at what he held up, her eyes widening as she inhaled sharply. "Oh, my."

His devilish smile sent her heart racing with excitement.

"Sweet angel, I think we'll start here."

THANK YOU for reading THE INNOCENT WIFE, Book Three of *Brides of Little Creede*. We hope you enjoyed Joshua and Vivian's story.

Did you miss reading Book One, THE SUBSTITUTE WIFE, Harrison's and Retta's story? Find out how it all began!

BUY LINK: https://www.amzn.com/B079Y95VY9/

And if you missed out on Frank and Catherine's story, in Book Two, THE DANCE HALL WIFE, you can find it here!

BUY LINK: https://www.amzn.com/B07FKP7L52/

Connect with CiCi Cordelia and her Alter Egos, Char Chaffin and Cheryl Yeko:

CiCi can be found on Facebook:
https://www.facebook.com/HeartfeltRomance
And on their website:
https://ccromance.com

Individually they are here:

Cheryl Yeko:

Website:
https://cherylyeko.blogspot.com/ 'Where Love Always Wins'
Amazon:
http://tinyurl.com/qzsks8q
Facebook:
https://www.facebook.com/WhereLoveAlwaysWins/

Twitter:
https://twitter.com/cherylyeko
Pinterest:
http://www.pinterest.com/cyeko/boards/
Goodreads:
http://www.goodreads.com/author/show/5406425.Cheryl_Yeko

Char Chaffin:

Website:
https://charbchaffin.wordpress.com 'Falling In Love is Only the Beginning'
Facebook:
http://facebook.com/char.chaffin
Amazon:
http://tinyurl.com/pvscu7w
Twitter:
http://twitter.com/char_chaffin
Goodreads:
http://www.goodreads.com/author/show/5337737.Char_Chaffin

Also from **Soul Mate Publishing** and **CiCi Cordelia**:

THE SUBSTITUTE WIFE
(Brides of Little Creede Book 1)

HARRISON . . .

Once his fortune in silver mining is secured, Harrison Carter finally sends back home for his fiancée. It's been four years since he's seen Jenny.

But it's Retta Pierce, Jenny's sister, who arrives by stagecoach with young daughter Adeline in tow. When this lovely, soiled dove brings devastating news and a written plea from Jenny to marry and care for Retta and little Addie, what's a good man to do?

RETTA . . .

Fulfilling her dying sister's request, Retta travels across dangerous territory to marry a man she barely remembers. But the hard miner who meets her at the stagecoach surely isn't the same one her sister claimed was kind and honorable, a gentleman who'll embrace her and her daughter as if they were his own. Has she made a mistake she'll pay for, the rest of her life?

TWO PEOPLE . . .

Thrown together in shared sorrow, Harrison and Retta struggle to forge a life in the brand-new state of late-nineteenth-century Colorado.

Now available on Amazon: THE SUBSITITUTE WIFE

THE DANCE HALL WIFE
(Brides of Little Creede Book 2)

CAT . . .

Cat Purdue has come a long way from the days when her father used her as partial payment for a gambling debt to a ruthless man. Reacquiring the saloon Father had lost, and turning it into a successful restaurant, is only the beginning of her drive for success.

FRANK . . .

Unable to reconcile the new, sophisticated Catherine Purdue from the saloon girl he once dallied with and foolishly spurned, Frank Carter finds himself blocking his growing attraction with sharp words and sarcasm. But when the Carters' old nemesis escapes prison and comes back to Little Creede for vengeance, Frank's only thought is to protect Cat, as well as his family.

A PAIR OF HEARTS . . .

Determined to lead separate lives yet bound together by danger and their growing desire, Frank and Cat will leave their mark in the new state of Colorado.

Now available on Amazon: **THE DANCE HALL WIFE**

CPSIA information can be obtained
at www.ICGtesting.com
Printed in the USA
BVHW041436160719
553594BV00012B/330/P

9 781682 918982